"You're a liar, mademoiselle," Luc said

His voice was full of dry derision. "Despite the prim-and-proper exterior, I reckon once you'd thawed out you'd give a man a run for his money. Being tied to a cripple for life wouldn't suit you at all."

"Well, as the question is hypothetical, I can't see that it matters," Elise retorted stormily, "because first, I'm not going to marry you, and second, I mean to get you out of that wheelchair."

The clash between them set the tone for the rest of the morning. The exercises, which Luc clearly regarded as a demeaning demonstration of his handicap, made him even more caustic and sarcastic.

Heels tapping smartly, Elise walked out of the room. Perhaps they both needed time to cool off. She'd never met anyone who could ruffle her the way Luc did.

Jenny Arden, a British writer, combines a
career as a college lecturer in business studies with
the writing she has always wanted to do. Her
favorite place for relaxation is North Wales, but
travel fascinates her—both the places she has
visited and the places she dreams about for future
journeying. In her spare time she enjoys sculpting
historical figures in clay and cooking for company.
Huckleberry, her Burmese Blue cat, is her
companion while writing. He usually sits in a chair
beside the typewriter, but occasionally, in a fit of
jealousy, will bid for her attention by sitting on
the keys!

Books by Jenny Arden

HARLEQUIN ROMANCE
2995—SOME ENCHANTING EVENING

Don't miss any of our special offers. Write to us at the
following address for information on our newest releases.

Harlequin Reader Service
901 Fuhrmann Blvd., P.O. Box 1397, Buffalo, NY 14240
Canadian address: P.O. Box 603,
Fort Erie, Ont. L2A 5X3

Intense Involvement

Jenny Arden

Harlequin Books

TORONTO • NEW YORK • LONDON
AMSTERDAM • PARIS • SYDNEY • HAMBURG
STOCKHOLM • ATHENS • TOKYO • MILAN

Original hardcover edition published in 1989
by Mills & Boon Limited

ISBN 0-373-03055-X

Harlequin Romance first edition June 1990

For Barbara,
friend and physio

CHAPTER ONE

IT FELT strange to Elise not to be wearing her white uniform when she was about to meet a new patient. But then always before she had worked in hospital. That made this job a double first for her: her first as a live-in physio and her first abroad.

She had arrived at the elegant château that was the property of the de Rozanieux family the day before. It was her first visit to the Loire valley but, despite that, the region, with its acres of vineyards and lush meadows, had seemed immediately to strike a chord in her, a response she supposed that had something to do with the fact that she was half-French.

Crossing the large drawing-room, she went to the long windows to gaze down the drive. Her auburn hair, burnished in the sunlight, was pinned up attractively, her fringe which parted slightly in the middle drawing attention to cool grey-green eyes that had a hint of hazel radiating out from their centres.

It was a lovely evening, almost summer, and her crisp cotton dress was a classic shirtwaister. There was nothing especially striking about it, yet with its collar raised so that the points framed her face and with her hands slipped casually into its side-seam pockets she gave it style. She looked brisk and self-sufficient, her image matching her personality. She had been twenty-one when she had decided to make her job her life. Now, with her emotions as well-ordered as her case notes, she had almost forgotten what it was like to be vulnerable, even if she had not forgotten what it was like to be hurt.

There was still no sign of Dr Dercourt's blue

Citroën. Through the partially open doors on to the hall she could hear the housekeeper giving a series of instructions to one of the maids. Evidently Brigitte wasn't satisfied with the preparations for dinner. For Luc de Rozanieux's first evening home everything had to be perfect.

The hospital at Montpierre had done as much as it could, and he was being discharged today in a wheelchair. The doctor had left for Montpierre with Fabienne, Luc's sister, almost an hour ago. At any moment they would be back.

Elise found she was curious about the man who was to be her patient. Fabienne had taken her on a tour of the estate that morning, showing her the vineyards and the château's winery, which produced some of the finest dry and sparkling wines of Touraine. Everyone Elise had been introduced to had paused first to ask Fabienne about Luc, clearly as delighted as she was that he was returning home today. It was plain that he inspired an almost feudal sense of loyalty in his staff.

Yet Dr Dercourt had said enough to make her prepared to meet an austere tyrant with a short temper. Having worked with Elise at Stoke Mandeville at one time, he had known he could afford to be honest with her. She wasn't the type to be put off by the prospect of an exacting patient—that was one of the reasons why he had recommended her to Fabienne. Another reason was that she had five years' experience in spinal injury treatment.

A small, dark-haired boy came running into the room. Six years old, he had alert brown eyes and an urchin-like thatch of dark hair. Elise, who was fond of children, had immediately taken to Luc's little nephew. Smiling at him, she asked, '*Qu'est-ce que tu veux, Michel?*'

'I hoped Uncle Luc would be here by now.'

'He will be soon. Any minute now you'll see the car.'

Michel nodded and then asked with a frown of puzzlement, 'Why can't Uncle Luc walk any more? *Maman* said the hospital would make him better.'

'The chances are that one day your uncle Luc will be able to walk again, but we've all got to be very patient. You see, when he was in that car crash he hurt his back very badly.' Elise half turned, placing her palm against her spine as she asked, 'Can you feel the bones you've got here?'

Michel copied her. Finding where his T-shirt had come untucked from his trousers, he nodded seriously.

'Well,' Elise continued, 'in the crash your uncle broke one of these bones. That hurt all the nerves, and nerves don't heal quickly.'

In fact her patient's injuries could easily have been far worse. If the accident had damaged the spinal cord there would have been no prospect at all of his walking again. As it was, only the nerve roots were affected. Since it depended on their capacity to regenerate it was too early for Dr Dercourt to predict precisely how extensive Luc's recovery was likely to be. Intensive therapy would help, and so would time. But for now he remained as he had ever since he had been in hospital, totally paralysed from the waist down.

'Why didn't Chantal hurt her back too?' Michel wanted to know.

Elise was about to ask who Chantal was when she realised she must have been Luc's passenger when his car had been crashed into by a drunken driver four times over the limit.

'She was very lucky,' Elise answered. 'Amazingly lucky.'

'Uncle Luc pulled her out of the car before it caught

fire,' Michel said proudly.

'Yes, I know,' said Elise. 'Dr Dercourt told me.'

Which was why her patient was paralysed now. In dragging his unconscious passenger to safety he had dislocated his fractured vertebrae, and it was that which had caused all the damage to the nerve endings.

At that moment the doctor's car drew up outside, its tyres crunching on the gravel. Michel's whole face lit up. Turning from the window, he raced into the hall, shouting, 'Brigitte, Brigitte, Uncle Luc's here!'

The sound of Michel's excited voice set the Alsatian which had been lying in the hall like a sentinel barking noisily. As the car doors opened, the dog, still barking furiously, bounded ahead of Michel down the shallow steps from the house. After them at a more sedate pace came the smiling housekeeper. Elise watched an instant longer, unable to catch more than a glimpse of her patient in the general confusion of welcome.

She went outside to help Dr Dercourt, who had lined up the wheelchair with the passenger door. Her view of the man in the car was still blocked, but she certainly heard him, as must everyone else remotely within earshot. Amid the hubbub of noise, he suddenly exploded, 'What is this—a reception committee? Fabienne, take Michel and go indoors. Brigitte, you as well. If there's one thing I don't need it's a damn audience while I demonstrate how useless my legs are!'

The mounting ferocity in his harsh baritone voice got prompt obedience. Only Michel protested in disappointment as his mother took hold of his hand.

'But I wanted . . .'

'Later, *chéri*,' Fabienne said quickly. 'Come on, let's go indoors now. Your uncle's tired.'

'But . . .'

'No buts,' she insisted firmly.

Obviously worried about her brother, she gave Elise a wan smile as she passed her on the steps before going into the house together with Michel and Brigitte.

Not at all intimidated by the man's angry outburst, Elise walked calmly to the car. With the minimum of assistance from the doctor, Luc hauled himself into the wheelchair. Dr Dercourt clicked the armrest back into place and automatically she bent down in front of the patient to adjust the footrests.

'Who the hell are you?'

The snap in the masterful voice compelled her to glance up. Anger and frustration were common reactions among paraplegics as they tried to come to terms with their disability. The man's tone didn't alter her readiness to be friendly and understanding.

Yet she found some of her compassion mysteriously fading as her eyes clashed with his. A faint prickling stirred at the back of her neck and her hand went to erase the sensation. She refused to allow a total stranger, however threateningly male, to make her feel in any way challenged.

She allowed her clinical gaze to flicker over him, taking in his tough, lean look that stemmed both from his hard physique and the flintiness of his face. His hair was straight, well-cut and so black that it seemed to have almost a midnight-blue sheen to it. There was not one thread of grey in it, although he was thirty-four.

His brows, too, were dark, adding an extra sternness to his patrician features. The sunlight made her aware of the attractive vertical grooves on either side of his firm mouth and the shallower lines beside and beneath his piercing blue eyes. They suggested he was a man with a sense of humour, though at present there was scant evidence of it.

He was wearing a blue shirt, the expensive cut of which couldn't hide the broad, flat muscles of his chest. The accident must have caused some wasting of his legs, yet in dark twill trousers his thighs looked every bit as hard as the rest of him. Even in a wheelchair, arrogance and virility seemed stamped in every line of him and, unsettled, even faintly antagonised, Elise got swiftly to her feet. She was relieved to find that, standing, she felt moderately less at a disadvantage.

'I'm Elise Sterling,' she informed him. 'I'll be taking over your physiotherapy treatment now that you're out of hospital.'

Her smile was pleasant, if a shade impersonal. It had no effect whatsoever on his hard stare. This was her second clash with those icy blue eyes. She never allowed her emotions to get out of check; it was a cardinal rule she had lived by for the past six years. As a result of it she seldom found herself either strongly attracted to, or antagonised by, a man, yet within the first few minutes of encountering Luc de Rozanieux her hackles were rising.

She had the vague comprehension that if she'd met him before the accident her reaction would have been even more intense. She could imagine what his lithe, tigerish walk would have been like. There was something animal about him, something dangerous, and if she'd met him socially her first instinct would have been to put as much of a safe distance between them as possible.

The doctor put a hand on Luc's shoulder as he said easily, 'Elise will be good for you. In fact, I'd almost lay odds that with therapy you'll regain quite a degree of feeling in your legs.'

'So that I can shuffle uselessly with a frame?' Luc queried with harsh contempt. His jawline was tight as, mastering his anger, he went on drily, 'Well, I suppose that would be preferable to this for life. Are you staying to dinner, Claude?'

'Thanks, I'd like to.'

'Then I'll leave it to you to tell Brigitte. And at the same time perhaps you'd tell Fabienne I'm resting,' Luc said a shade tersely. 'I've no particular wish to be burdened with the solicitous care of my family just now. The physio can see me to my room.'

'Don't shut your family out, Luc,' Dr Dercourt said with measured gravity. 'They want to help, that's all.'

'Stick to medical advice, Doctor!' Luc fired back.

His voice had the ring of steel to it, and there was a glint of cynical amusement in his eyes. Claude Dercourt was both his doctor and his friend. Luc knew him too well to expect to be subjected to his bedside manner.

Glancing at the Alsatian, which had dropped down on its haunches near the wheelchair, Claude commented rather drily, 'I'm surprised Nikki isn't out of favour too.'

'I'm not averse to loyalty, merely pity,' Luc said harshly, a bitter twist to his mouth.

Dr Dercourt gave an inaudible sigh. Then, clicking his fingers to Nikki, who came towards him, he said, 'Well, I'll leave you for the moment in Elise's care. I know you'll want to get acquainted with her.'

Luc's contemptuous silence suggested otherwise. Judging it best to say no more, the doctor strolled towards the house, the Alsatian at his heels.

'So you're the wonder-worker,' Luc said derisively as finally he bothered to direct a comment to Elise.

Determined to be treated with at least the conventional amount of civility, she said calmly, 'If you missed my name, Monsieur de Rozanieux, it's——'

'I heard it the first time,' he snarled, 'or do you

think I'm deaf as well as crippled?'

What she was starting to think, but refrained from saying so, was that he was insufferably rude. She was about to take hold of the handles of the wheelchair when she was ordered fiercely, 'I'll tell you when I want your assistance!'

'If that's what you prefer,' she murmured smoothly, taking a steadying breath.

She had the strongest suspicion that his temper was only perilously contained. She wasn't going to cross him needlessly. In any case, although she didn't warm to the man, his obstinate refusal to accept help merited a certain respect.

'You're not what I was expecting,' he stated, not as a compliment, as he propelled himself along. 'You look fragile enough to break.'

She was certain the challenge in the comment was deliberate and, mildly provoked by it, she told him, 'I'm not made of porcelain. I can assure you I've manhandled men every bit as big as you before now.'

A nerve jumped in his cheek. His hands pushed savagely at the large wheels as he answered with jeering sarcasm, 'You're a real advertisement for English femininity, *mademoiselle*. I'm sure you're going to brighten up my life no end!'

Elise resisted the impulse to rise to the taunt. Damn the man, he was already making her feel snappy when she was trying her hardest to appear brisk and pleasant! Pretending to have missed the derision, she took hold of the handles of the wheelchair and said quite cheerfully, 'I hope so.'

'I said I didn't need your help, damn you!' he exploded.

The force in his voice made her start. What was even more maddening was that she almost leapt unthinking to his command. Subduing her annoyance, she said equably, 'Propelling a wheelchair unaided up a ramp takes practice. You're probably not aware of it, but the paralysis in your legs will have altered your whole sense of balance. If you tipped forward and fell, it would be my fault.'

She heard his infuriated muttered oath, though even if she hadn't she would have known that he was raging at being even temporarily dependent on her. She could see it in the brute tension in his shoulders. Hoping to placate him, she went on amiably, 'A bedroom's been made for you downstairs. With its own bathroom en suite, you'll be completely self-contained . . .'

'For heaven's sake, spare me the bright hospital manner,' he said cuttingly.

'Monsieur de Rozanieux,' she answered briskly, 'I understand your frustration——'

'Do you?' he interrupted, a trace of bitter humour in his voice as he added, 'Frankly, I very much doubt it.'

The nerve that jumped again along his jaw suggested that he felt even more violent than he sounded. Thinking it wisest not to contradict him, Elise wheeled him across the château's marble-floored hall into his room.

Even with its orthopaedic bed, bedside telephone and remote-control switches for the television and CD player, it retained an air of old-world elegance. French windows framed a restful view of terrace, gardens and swimming pool. The antique furniture blended well with the two square modern armchairs, and the whole room gave an impression of light and spaciousness.

Leaving Luc's side, Elise walked over to the bed. With the touch of a switch she raised the back of it to a sloping angle, remarking as she did so, in an attempt to rekindle some form of conversation,

'Montpierre's a very pretty town. In my free time I thought I'd explore it.'

She turned back to face him in time to see his eyes lift from her slim legs in their champagne-coloured stockings. There was not one flicker of apology in his hard gaze for his blatant masculine scrutiny, and to her intense annoyance she felt herself colour. She couldn't think how long it was since a man, let alone a patient, had made her blush, and her voice was a shade cool as she said, 'Do you need any help to get from the wheelchair on to the bed?'

'Use your imagination!' he ground back.

'There's no need to be sarcastic.'

'Is the Florence Nightingale act wearing thin already?' he mocked, raising his dark brows slightly.

Elise glared at him before remembering that, however difficult a patient might be, her job was to establish a rapport between them so they could work together successfully. Swallowing her animosity, she said with forced calm, 'I'm not here to be your nurse.' She pushed him towards the bed, and then went on, 'Now, first of all, in any transfer remember to set the brake so the chair can't roll. Then grip the armrest with one hand and place the other on the mattress. That's going to give you the leverage to lift you on to the bed. Are you ready to try it?'

'And what are you going to do while I perform this feat?' asked Luc with light irony.

She had the strong suspicion that her unexpected flash of temper had amused him in a wry sort of way. But he certainly wasn't going to be rewarded by seeing it twice. She was much too cool and professional for that.

'I'm going to watch and see how you get on,' she said pleasantly.

'I thought your aim was not to have me fall,' he observed drily.

'You won't fall, not if you follow my instructions,' she assured him, before adding, 'You need to grip the armrest a little further back, Monsieur de Rozanieux.'

Taking hold of his wrist, she placed his left hand in the correct position, curving his tanned fingers round the armrest. Her heart seemed to skip a beat with the physical contact, making her feel unreasonably defensive. She found that her eyes were drawn to Luc's shirt, which was open at the throat, exposing the swarthy column of his neck and revealing a shading of dark hair on his chest.

Her every instinct at that moment was to retreat from him. Caged tigers, she thought, had the same quality of latent, pent-up, dangerous energy as this man exuded. A shiver seemed to run over her skin, an alien sensation she didn't like one bit, and, if only because of it, she stubbornly held her ground.

'Now, push yourself up and twist on to the bed,' she said, outwardly at least all calm composure.

'If you want me to do that,' he said, mocking her, 'you're going to have to give me more room.'

Quickly she took a step back, impatient with herself for obstructing him, and thankful that he didn't know the reason for it. Then, as he began to attempt the transfer, the physio in her made her forget her reaction to him.

She watched him attentively, ready to assist him if necessary. But he needed no help. With his mouth compressed to a stern line, he hoisted his weight out of the wheelchair. He was a good six feet tall, and the muscles bunched in his powerful arms as he swung his body on to the bed with something of the grace of an athlete.

'You did that . . .' she began, before remembering that he was not particularly taken with her bright hospital manner. It was too late anyway to halt in mid-sentence, so she completed it, 'You did that very well.'

'I'll live on your praise for at least a week,' he said sarcastically, adding as, leaning forward, he hauled first one paralysed leg and then the other on to the bed, 'You certainly don't believe in pampering anyone, do you?'

'I imagine you had enough of that in hospital, especially after six weeks of it. Besides, I'm not here to pamper you. I'm here to try and help you to be as independent as possible,' she answered.

'Quite a tall order when my legs are paralysed,' he said, his voice clipped.

'Not if the way you swung yourself out of that wheelchair just now is anything to go by,' she disagreed.

He leaned back, surveying her leisurely for a moment before saying, 'So what other treats have you got lined up for me?'

Elise was glad that some of his hostility towards her seemed to be fading, even if she couldn't honestly say the same. Luc de Rozanieux was just too blatantly and arrogantly male for her liking. She couldn't explain it, but he unsettled her, and even now that he was giving her a respite from his angry sarcasm she suspected he was still mocking her crisp, efficient tone.

Refusing to let him get under her skin, she answered, 'We'll start with some circulation and balancing exercises. You'll need some more practice with manoeuvring the wheelchair. Tomorrow I'll set up an obstacle course for you. You'll also want me to teach you how to dress yourself . . .'

'You're not my damned nurse!' he interrupted shortly.

His eyes, so arrestingly blue against his tanned skin, demanded a retraction from her. She might have guessed that her proposal would hit his male pride, but there was no way he was bullying her into not doing her job properly. She said with a faint note of challenge, 'Do you have some problem with accepting dressing help from a woman?'

'Let's just say I'm more used to undressing a woman than having her dress me,' he replied, letting his raking gaze slide over her.

His considering expression made her feel a flush of heat that spread upwards into her face. She took a quick intake of breath, momentarily at a loss, before managing to say with unmistakable emphasis, 'I can promise you, this is one woman you won't be undressing! Not even with your eyes!'

Luc's gaze returned to her face. With deliberately overdone casualness he asked, 'Do you have some problem with accepting attention from a man?'

For an angry instant she felt she would choke on his mockery. Not wanting him to have the satisfaction of seeing it, she averted her face, making a pretence of checking that the carafe of water was within easy reach on the bedside table. Not till she was sure her voice would sound unruffled did she announce, 'There, I think you have everything you need, Monsieur de Rozanieux. I'll leave you to rest for a while.'

She was on her way to the door when she was halted with the barked command, 'You're staying right here until I say otherwise. Sit down!'

She wheeled sharply. His domineering manner went beyond anything she'd encountered in her work before.

'I don't take orders from patients,' she corrected him rather tartly.

'Then indulge me. I said sit down!'

It annoyed her than he should assume his will was strong enough to override hers, yet just the same she dropped into the nearest armchair. Seeing the faintly stormy light that had come into her eyes, he mocked gently, 'Am I taxing your temper, *mademoiselle*?'

'If that's your aim, you'll be disappointed,' she answered with stoical calm.

'You're quite the model of cool composure, aren't you?' he sneered. 'Pity your personality hasn't a bit of fire, like your looks.'

'I'm not the remotest bit interested in your criticism of my looks or personality,' Elise shot back.

Dr Dercourt had been right when he had warned her that this case was going to be difficult. Luc de Rozanieux was already managing to strike sparks off her when normally nothing ever ruffled her clinical composure. She wanted to feel pity for him, yet there was something about his hard-chiselled features and the arrogant flare of his nostrils that defied pity. He was altogether too ferocious a man to instil compassion in her.

'It wasn't your looks I was criticising,' he answered, a lazier note coming into his voice. 'As it happens, I've always had a penchant for green-eyed redheads. Especially ones who blush at the thought of being undressed.'

His comment made it somehow take an immense degree of determination for Elise to continue to meet his gaze. She was so used to feeling completely in control of every situation that it annoyed her to find that Luc could fluster her so easily.

With a composure she was far from feeling, she said, 'Don't think you can discomfit me with remarks like that. I've worked with enough male patients for that particular line of repartee no longer to make any impact on me.'

Her put-down had no effect, apart from bringing a faint cynical amusement into his eyes.

'That's easy enough to believe,' he said

disparagingly. 'I suppose you save what faint embers of warmth there are in your nature for the doctors.'

'I'm afraid I don't follow you.'

'Naïveté doesn't suit you,' he said. 'It's absolutely obvious you talked Claude into recommending you.'

For an instant she stared at him. Then she spluttered, affronted, 'Talked him into recommending me? I did no such thing! *He* contacted *me* about this job, and asked me if I was interested.'

'And you were interested all right,' sneered Luc. 'After all, what better way to make a play for the good doctor?'

Indignation no less strong in her voice, despite her incredulous breath of laughter, she exclaimed, 'How dare you? How *dare* you imply that I'm chasing Dr Dercourt?'

The icy cynicism in Luc's eyes told her he was unimpressed by her denial.

'I wish you the best of luck, Mademoiselle Sterling,' he said with abrasive mockery. 'A widower for eight years, and with your work in common—you should be in with a good chance.'

'Let me tell you something,' she said. 'I admire Claude Dercourt as a brilliant and dedicated doctor. But I didn't even know until you told me just now that he happens to be a widower. I took this job solely because I wanted some experience outside a hospital.'

'Is that so?'

Luc's clipped tone poured scorn on her vehement denial and, finding it hard to keep hold of her temper, she retorted, 'Yes, that's exactly so.'

'And of course, even if he were to ask you to marry him, you'd turn him down, along with his money,' Luc drawled with scorn.

Simmering with animosity and no longer able to hide it, Elise exclaimed, 'You leave me speechless!'

'Or have I touched you on the raw?'

'Being confined to a wheelchair doesn't give you the right to insult me!'

There was a sudden nerve-tensing silence. Luc's nostrils flared. With one hand he gripped the side of the bed, the knuckles showing white, as though by sheer force of will he could get to his feet.

'If you're going to stay here, you'll damn well watch your tongue,' he said between clenched teeth.

'You mean you don't mind handing out insults, but you don't like getting any back.'

With a little flicker of alarm Elise suddenly realised that not many people dared speak to this man as she was now doing. His mouth was thinned to a savage line and he looked capable of violence. Even though she knew he couldn't cross the room to shake an apology out of her, she suddenly had to clench her hands to stop them from trembling.

Yet she had no intention of climbing down. Luc would dismiss her instructions out of hand unless he had some measure of respect for her, and she would never win that from him if she showed she could be cowed by his temper. With fighting spirit she went on, 'You're angry because you can't walk——'

'How sharp of you to notice!' he cut across her with scathing sarcasm.

'Then work with me and do something about it! Because that would be far more constructive than lashing out at everyone.'

Luc's mouth tightened. Then he leaned his head back against the pillow, closing his eyes as though she wearied him. His voice was sardonic and dry as he said, 'I'm sure countless patients have responded to that rallying tone of yours. You'll have to forgive me if I prefer to face facts, and those are that even with therapy I'm likely to remain a cripple.'

'That's a word you seem to like,' she observed.

His eyes opened to transfix her with icy cynicism.

'And you, I suppose, prefer the term paraplegic? From where I am, the meaning's the same.'

Elise paused, considering him with her cool gaze. Then she said, the note of challenge in her voice deliberate, 'It's strange, when I met you at the car I wouldn't have labelled you as a defeatist.'

'For heaven's sake, don't patronise me!' he snarled. 'Your damned prissy manner's enough to put up with!'

'I don't much like your manner, either,' she returned.

'Get used to it, because there's going to be a hell of a lot more that you don't like.'

'What I dislike most of all is your self-pitying attitude,' she said crisply.

A tremor of apprehension went through her as Luc's nostrils flared. It didn't seem possible that she could go on saying these things and get away with them. But she had already realised that gentle encouragement wasn't going to get her anywhere with a man like Luc. Her only hope of working successfully with him was to capitalise on his rage and frustration, getting him to put that bull-like energy into his programme of therapy. If in the process it seemed as if he would like to tear her limb from limb she would just have to ignore his caustic comments.

His blue eyes glinted as he stared at her. Then in an ominously quiet voice he said, 'I'm surprised someone hasn't put you in your place before now, Mademoiselle Sterling.'

Curling her fingers into her palms, Elise returned his gaze, her voice completely even as she said, 'I was thinking exactly the same about you.'

'Tell me,' he drawled with a derisive intonation,

'does it give you some kind of satisfaction to be in a position where you can boss a man around? Is it a compensation for being a single, frustrated twenty-seven?'

'If your remarks about undressing women are anything to go by,' she answered, '*you're* the one suffering from frustration.'

'You bitch!' he said on a breath of amused contempt.

'I object to being sworn at,' she told him stonily.

'I would have thought a pain in the neck like you would have been used to it.'

'And I would have thought that a gentleman doesn't become a boor the moment his virility is called into question.'

For a frightening instant Elise thought from his reaction that she'd gone too far. Luc shot her a savage look from under lowered dark brows, every muscle in his face taut with anger.

'I ought to throw you out for that remark!' he snarled.

'You won't have to,' she said, striving to keep her voice firm, 'because I'm not staying to listen to any more.'

'You don't quit till I fire you!' he thundered in such a hurricane of a mood that her heart started thudding unevenly.

Hating its hammering and the sudden dryness of her mouth, she answered promptly, 'Quit? Who said anything about quitting? I've no intention of leaving this house until you're on your feet again. Or didn't Dr Dercourt tell you when he recommended me that I *never* give up on a challenge?'

Luc kept his hard stare on her. His face was still set in ruthless lines, but his eyes no longer glittered with rage.

'Does that also apply to the doctor himself?' he

asked gratingly.

'I've already told you I'm not here to inveigle anyone into marriage,' she almost snapped at him. 'It's up to you whether you choose to listen or not.'

Pivoting sharply, she turned and walked from the room.

CHAPTER TWO

HER COURT shoes tapping smartly on the marble floor, Elise crossed the hall. Directly opposite her was a large gilt-framed mirror, an ornate Sèvres vase massed with carnations and roses set on the mahogany table in front of it.

Catching sight of her reflection above the flowers, she saw that her slim straightness held a touch of uncharacteristic defiance. Even her eyes, usually so cool, were a turbulent green. She paused, drawing a long breath. Her patient had ruffled her composure more than she had realised. Forcing herself to cool down, she went into the drawing-room.

Fabienne was sitting on the sofa talking to the doctor. Her elbow rested on the sofa's arm, a thin spiral of smoke rising from the cigarette she held in her fingers. Hearing Elise's step, she glanced up sharply.

'How did you get on?' she asked quickly.

'I'm surprised you didn't hear the shouting,' Elise said, putting humour into her voice.

Fabienne was under enough strain without having to worry over the fact that she and Luc hadn't clicked. The dark brown hair that framed her face made her look pale and there were faint shadows of fatigue under her eyes.

'I'm afraid Luc's in one devil of a mood at the moment,' she said hopelessly as she leant forward to tap ash from her cigarette.

'Contrary to what's sometimes said,' Dr Dercourt commented, 'people just aren't at their best when they're ill. Adjusting to this sort of disability is always

26

difficult. And for a man as assertive and independent as Luc it's bound to be extra hard.'

'He seems so angry,' Fabienne sighed.

'That's not necessarily a bad thing,' said Elise. 'With a lot of patients you have to keep coaxing them. They need constant encouragement if they're to learn to be independent, and it's an uphill task all the way. I'm not going to have that problem with your brother. All I have to do is to suggest I help him, and he looks as if he'd like to murder me!'

Dr Dercourt chuckled at her description.

'Yes, I can imagine. Still, I know I don't have to tell you not to let him bully you. I wanted you on this case because I was sure you'd stand up to him.'

Fabienne paced over to the french windows and stood staring out over the lawns where Michel was playing with Nikki in the evening sunlight. Claude's astute diagnostic gaze swung to her.

'Relax, Fabienne,' he said, his voice kind yet authoritative. 'You've got Luc home from hospital; Elise is here to start his programme of therapy, and now you can think about Michel and your boutique and go on with rebuilding your life.'

Fabienne turned abruptly.

'It's all very well to talk,' she said sharply, 'but no, everything is not as rosy as you're painting it. Luc's embittered and depressed, and I can't get through to him. He's been like this for weeks now. He rejects me when I want to help.'

'He's rejecting everyone at the moment,' Elise said gently. 'It's not just you.'

'Try to be patient, Fabienne,' Dr Dercourt advised.

'Patience isn't the problem,' she answered. 'Of course I can be patient. What I don't like is feeling so useless. When Rémy collapsed suddenly last year I was frantic. I phoned Luc from the hospital and immediately he was in his car and on his way to

Paris.' Her voice caught a little as she went on, 'From that moment he took over everything for me, arranging the funeral, selling the flat, bringing me and Michel here and then helping me buy the boutique in town. He was there for me when I needed him. So why am I being so useless now that the situation is reversed? Why is it there's not a thing I can do to bring him out of this mood of angry depression?'

'You can't expect to,' Elise explained. 'Not all at once. All patients go through periods of anger and depression.'

Dr Dercourt rubbed a thoughtful finger along his cheek.

'I think the best way for you to help him, Fabienne,' he said, 'is to try and treat him as if the car crash had never happened. Now that he's home, why don't you resume managing the boutique again?'

'How can I when there's the vineyard to run? Even with the bailiff seeing to most of it, it's a full-time job.'

'Let Luc see to it.'

'But surely he shouldn't be worried with problems just now,' she protested.

'I'm hoping he'll want to be in charge again,' Dr Dercourt answered. 'Luc's a businessman. It's been his personal direction and control that's made the vineyard renowned in the area. Of course, he mustn't overdo things for a while yet, but if he could take over some of the work it might stop him brooding.'

Fabienne walked over to the coffee table and stubbed out her cigarette.

'Well, I can suggest it,' she agreed. She smiled ruefully. 'What would I do if I didn't have you to listen to all my problems?'

'But you do have me,' the doctor replied with a touch of banter.

'In which case, since everything is to go on as normal, will you excuse me while I persuade my son it's time for his bath?'

The doctor laughed.

'Of course.'

Elise waited till she had gone out and then commented, 'She's taking it very hard.'

'Yes, she is,' Dr Dercourt agreed soberly. 'In fact, you'll probably need to be a bit of a psychiatrist for Fabienne as well as a physio for Luc. For her to lose her husband and then to have her brother paralysed all in under a year has been a lot for her to cope with.'

'How old was her husband when he died?'

'Still in his thirties. That was what was so tragic. He had a heart attack. It was completely without warning. He was a barrister. One day he came home after a successful session in court and just collapsed. For Fabienne it was the most dreadful shock. No woman expects to be widowed at twenty-eight.'

'So that was why she came back home,' said Elise.

'Yes. Rémy's only relation was a brother in Martinique. It would have made no sense for her to stay in Paris. Besides, for a while she went totally to pieces. Luc was wonderfully supportive, and setting her up in a boutique was exactly what she needed.'

'Did he always have a wild temper?' she asked, trying to understand her patient a little better. 'I mean, even before the accident?'

'Luc could always cut people down to size,' the doctor said with a trace of dry humour. 'You'd be unique if you weren't the target of at least some of his sarcasm.'

'To be honest with you,' she confessed, 'I wouldn't be surprised if he fires me before the week's out. I don't intend holding the candle to him, but I'm sure not many people answer him back and get away with it.'

'Luc won't fire you,' the doctor answered, speaking with assurance, 'because he knows you're his best chance of walking again. The only question is, how do *you* feel about being shouted at round the clock?'

'I'll survive it,' she said, her chin lifting. She went on, refusing to be daunted, 'In fact, I like it here. Fabienne's made me feel so welcome, and Michel is a darling.'

'I understand from Fabienne that you're quite a favourite with him too.' The doctor smiled, before commenting, 'I'm surprised you're such a single-minded career woman when you've such a natural way with children.'

'I obviously never met the right man,' she lied lightly, with no evidence of the dart of pain she felt.

Immediately she pushed the pang away. There was no point in wishing that things had worked out differently. Richard had stopped loving her, and surely it was better that he had realised it before their wedding than after it? Wanting to change the subject, she said, 'I thought I'd start off tomorrow with a two-hour session of therapy in the morning and another in the afternoon.'

The conversation shifted from Luc to the doctor's work at the hospital. It stayed with medical matters in general until the door opened and Michel and Fabienne came in.

The little boy was in his pyjamas, his dark hair still damp from the shower.

'I've just been showing Uncle Luc my new stamps from Martinique,' he announced happily. '*Maman* said I could go in and say goodnight to him before I went to bed.'

'And now it's time you said goodnight to Dr

Dercourt and Elise as well,' said Fabienne.

'Must I go to bed now?' Michel protested appealingly.

'Yes, you must.'

'What did your uncle think of your stamps?' Dr Dercourt asked.

'He liked them,' said Michel. 'I told him Elise has promised to save the ones she gets on her letters from England for me. I've already got some in my collection, but now I'll have even more. Do you want to see them?'

'Another time,' Fabienne declared, familiar with her son's delaying tactics. Taking hold of him by the shoulders, she pointed him in the direction of the door.

As he went out, she remarked to Elise, 'Your being here seems to be making a difference already. Luc was quite his old self with Michel just now.'

'I don't think I can take the credit for that,' Elise disclaimed, thinking of Luc's hostility towards her.

It was almost half an hour later when Brigitte came in to announce that dinner was ready. Elise assumed that since Luc had invited Dr Dercourt to stay he intended joining them for the meal, but he would need help to come to the table.

She went and tapped on his door. Braced to receive more of his sarcasm, she went into his room. Then she stopped abruptly, concern coming into her eyes as she saw that the room was empty, and his wheelchair gone from the side of his bed. The french windows on to the terrace were open, the white net curtains billowing slightly in the breeze.

The stubborn fool, she thought. Hadn't he bothered to listen when she'd explained quietly about the risk of falling? Or did he simply intend countermanding whatever she said? Parting the fluttering net curtains, she went outside.

The sun had sunk low, bathing the white tufa limestone walls of the château in its warm golden glow. In contrast, the flowers of the clematis that trailed over the stone balustrade were a vibrant mauve, and further splashes of deep colour were provided by the geraniums and petunias that filled the classical stone urns.

Nikki was lying beside his master, his dark, pointed nose resting on his tan paws. Though she had stepped out on to the terrace noiselessly, immediately the dog raised his head, a low, menacing growl sounding deep in his throat. Luc, who had been staring grimly ahead, pivoted his chair round.

Noting the slightly wary glance Elise gave the powerful Alsatian, he jeered contemptuously, 'I thought you English were supposed to like animals? Nikki, be quiet!'

'Your dog's never growled at me like that before,' she defended herself. 'He must sense that you don't like me.'

'Alsatians are very intelligent,' Luc said caustically. He paused and then commented sarcastically, 'I was expecting some cheery comment to the effect that we'd both come round to you in the end.'

'You wouldn't listen to such a comment even if I made it,' she answered, 'just as you ignored me when I told you your sense of balance is disturbed and if you attempted to do too much by yourself you could fall.'

'Yes, I wheeled myself out here alone,' he snapped in agreement. 'What did you expect me to do? Lie meekly in bed until you fussed in to get me up?'

'I don't fuss,' she corrected him. She caught the faint drift of fragrance from a late-blossoming lilac and, hoping to call a truce, she went on, 'It's such a beautiful evening. At home at this time of year it's still blustery and cold.'

'Yes, we're lucky,' he answered drily. 'It's very mild here. But I'm sure you've heard the local saying, "On St Vincent's Day winter loses its teeth".'

His slight excess of politeness parodied her trite remarks about the weather. Determined not to allow him to nettle her, Elise ignored his rebuff and persevered amiably, 'Who's St Vincent?'

'He's the patron saint of wine-growers.'

'Then it must be his statue that's in the square at Montpierre. I wondered who——'

'I don't like chattering women,' Luc cut across her shortly.

'Only undressing them,' she snapped back, losing patience.

A cynical gleam came into his blue eyes, making her wish she hadn't spoken.

'That comment seems to be playing on your mind,' he mocked. 'Is it because it's some time since a man's given you that pleasure?'

She felt as if she was colouring, and hoped intensely that she wasn't. How was it he could make her blush so easily? She said a shade coolly, 'My sex life isn't your concern, Monsieur de Rozanieux. Now, as dinner's ready, I'd like to help you to the table.'

'I shan't be joining you.'

The curt statement told her that the matter wasn't open to discussion.

'But you have to eat,' she protested.

'If I'm hungry, I'll eat later in my room.'

'Eating alone isn't recommended to give anyone an appetite. And it's most important——'

'I'm not in the mood for dinner-table conversation,' he interrupted with curbed force, 'so you can make my apologies.'

Elise was getting a little tired both of being ordered around and of being cut short in mid-sentence when her sole concern was for his well-being.

'You can make your apologies yourself,' she answered briskly, 'because *I'm* not going to excuse your rudeness when Brigitte has gone to so much trouble with the meal.'

Luc's mouth thinned. She noted the way his fingers dug into the arms of his wheelchair as he said, 'If I ever get on my feet again, it's going to give me the greatest pleasure to see you to the station.'

'Does that mean you've changed your mind about joining us?' she asked.

'It seems I've little choice,' he snapped, keeping his implacably hard stare on her.

Forcing herself to meet it, she said boldly, 'Fabienne seems to think that the two of us are getting on reasonably well. For myself, I can put up with your temper, but as she's worried about you, I'd rather she wasn't completely disillusioned over dinner.'

'Is it my sister you're concerned about, or the impression you hope to make on Claude?' sneered Luc.

'I've already told you,' she exclaimed, 'I'm not trying to make an impression on Dr Dercourt!'

'Not even as the caring physio?' he mocked.

'I happen to care a great deal about my patients,' she told him. 'It's not some act I put on for the doctors' benefit, or for anyone else's, for that matter.'

'How reassuring!'

'Why don't you decide to be pleasant for a change?' she demanded. 'It wouldn't kill you not to jump down my throat every time I make a remark!'

'Then try making fewer of them,' Luc fired back sarcastically as he pivoted the wheelchair round with a capable hand. 'It would help me no end when it comes to being pleasant at dinner.'

With a vehement push he propelled himself away

from her towards the french windows. Elise
followed, annoyed to find that she was glaring at his
broad back and dark head of hair. She simply must
not allow the sparks of antipathy between them to
develop into a major problem.

Anticipating that dinner was going to be a strain,
she found the convivial atmosphere was a welcome
surprise. Evidently Luc had agreed to call a cease-fire
of sorts, and it helped, too, that in the doctor's
company Fabienne seemed less anxious and more
relaxed.

As the sparkling white wine was poured, Luc's
sister announced, 'I thought tonight we'd celebrate
with some of our special *cuvée.*'

'An idea I heartily approve of,' agreed Claude with
a smile.

'Let's hope it won't be wasted on Mademoiselle
Sterling,' Luc remarked, a sardonic joke in his voice.
Addressing Elise, he went on, 'As you're English——'

'Half-English,' she reminded him.

His mouth quirked ironically as he conceded the
point.

'But in any event,' he said, 'better qualified, I
imagine, to give me your opinion of a cup of
Darjeeling tea than a glass of the château's wine.'

Though the mockery in his voice was urbane, Elise
saw the icy derision in his blue eyes. He only had to
slash her with his gaze for her to itch to retaliate. But
she ignored the hidden jeer, seeming merely to tease
him in return as she challenged, 'So you'd like my
opinion?'

'I'm waiting eagerly.'

Intent on establishing that she wasn't the philistine
he seemed to think, she tilted her glass away from
her, assessing the wine's delicate colour against the
background of the white tablecloth. A stream of tiny
bubbles rose evenly to the surface, a hallmark of the

best sparkling wines. Then, giving her glass a quick twirl by its stem to release the wine's fragrance, she held her nose to it, before taking a generous considering sip.

'I'd say this is a Chenin Blanc with a honeyed nose and a crisp, stylish palate,' she said. 'It's vivacious and fruity, well-balanced and perfect for a celebration.'

'Bravo!' Claude laughed appreciatively. 'You certainly know your wine!'

'I have to admit I'm impressed,' Luc drawled in agreement, his eyes narrowing thoughtfully on her face. 'Where did you learn to be such a connoisseur?'

Elise's gaze faltered. Suddenly she wished intently that she hadn't let him provoke her into this game of bravado. She wouldn't have done if she'd guessed the conversation would lead to Richard. With a sense of despair she felt her throat tighten. She didn't know if it was the result of Luc's barrage of caustic sarcasm, but her emotions seemed all at once quite dangerously close to the surface.

'I used to know someone who worked for a wine merchant,' she said as casually as she could. 'He talked a lot about his job.'

'An old boyfriend?' Fabienne asked with a smile.

'A patient,' Elise answered misleadingly, though it wasn't a lie. Richard had needed treatment for a knee injury, which was how she had met him. She went on with a pretence of brightness, 'One of the interesting things about being a physio is coming into contact with so many different walks of life.'

'I think that's true with all medical work,' Claude agreed, and she realised thankfully that the conversation had shifted away from her.

It was only as she happened to glance up that she saw Luc watching her assessingly. A faint defensive prickling ran over her skin. It was ridiculous to suppose that he could have guessed anything from the timbre of her voice, but, even if he had, her broken engagement was something she never discussed with anyone. In her experience, hurt was best buried deep.

Keeping his word to be more civil, Luc used nothing harsher than the weapon of his mockery against her over dinner. Ironically there seemed to be almost a vibrancy in the electricity between them, instead of the clash of temperaments it masked—a clash, she reminded herself, that somehow she was going to have to resolve.

Fabienne suggested that they take their coffee into the drawing-room, where the conversation turned to the vineyard. Elise, who had been fascinated by her tour of the estate, was interested to hear Fabienne talk about the spring racking and the bottling that was now going on with the wines that had reached their prime condition.

She wasn't aware immediately that Luc was taking no part in the discussion. His indifference to the work that had gone on in his absence puzzled her, when Dr Dercourt had said that he'd always been personally involved in every aspect of the running of the vineyard.

She flickered a glance at him, studying him without seeming to as she tried to make sense of his stony detachment. His straight dark brows were drawn together slightly and, as always, there was something fierce in his icy blue eyes. Yet his face was an impassive mask. She could read nothing in it to help her guess his thoughts.

As Fabienne began to serve more coffee he said brusquely, 'No more for me.' He paused, his jawline tight despite the note of dry humour he put in his voice as he added, 'I'm afraid I'm tired, and I'm sure my physio would recommend bed as the best place for me. So if you'll excuse me, I'll say goodnight.'

He pushed his chair away from the coffee table, and Elise stood up to open the double doors for him as he wheeled himself from the room. Seeing the muscle that jumped in his tanned cheek, she realised just how close his anger was to exploding, despite the sociable way he'd made his excuses.

Surely *she* hadn't said something to annoy him? She couldn't think of anything. She had been so careful, but then it seemed it didn't take much for her to grate on his nerves.

She knew that he had been prescribed codeine. He hadn't said he was in pain, though after the drive home and several transfer movements it was quite likely that his back was giving him some trouble. But, whatever the cause of his displeasure, it was probably wiser not to trail him to his den until he'd simmered down.

As it was, her appearance seemed too soon for his liking. He had finished with the bathroom and was wheeling himself back into his room as Elise entered it. He had discarded his shirt, and her heart seemed to jolt a little at the sight of his naked chest with its tangle of dark hair.

'You're becoming like my damned shadow,' he greeted her derisively, his blue eyes contemptuous.

It was ridiculous when she was so used to seeing male patients stripped off that she should suddenly feel too closely confined with him. She saw that the muscles of his broad shoulders were full and rounded, almost as if they had been carved from teak, while those of his chest were broad and flat like his stomach. Just his blatant maleness seemed to antagonise her unreasonably. Subduing her response to him, she said amiably, 'For as long as you need me, I'm afraid that's the way it has to be.'

'So now what?' he growled, sarcasm coming into

his voice as he said harshly, 'Don't tell me. You've come to undress me and put me to bed.'

'I've come to *help* you to get undressed,' she corrected him.

'You seem to have a thwarted maternal instinct.'

'I'm simply doing my job,' she reminded him, then promptly chided herself for the perceptible edge of sharpness in her tone. He just seemed to have a gift, this man, for annoying her. She went on, determined to remain pleasant, 'If you'll transfer on to the bed, I'll help you to finish undressing and then we'll work through some passive movements——'

'The emphasis being on the word "passive"?' he asked harshly as he cut across her.

'For now, yes. Any programme of exercises has to be built up gradually. Until you've regained some sensation and power in your legs——'

'Which could be never,' he cut in.

'Then you'll have a devil of a long time to put up with me, won't you?' Elise retaliated.

Now she'd really done it, she thought, exasperated with herself. That incautious comment was bound to put a match to the charged atmosphere between them. But, instead of the savage anger she had expected, Luc merely gave a grunt of amused contempt. His cynical gaze stayed on her an instant before he hauled himself on to the bed with the dry comment, 'What a prospect for us both to look forward to!'

She drew a quick steadying breath, needing to be at her most calm and professional as she told him, 'Undo your belt and I'll show you how to take your trousers off.'

'Did I hear you right?' he asked levelly, quirking a dark brow at her.

'While you've been in hospital you haven't had to worry about things like getting into your pyjamas by yourself. But now you're home, the more independent you can be, the better,' she explained briskly. 'I'll only need to show you once. The rest is practice.'

'You're damned right about that,' he growled as his hand went to the buckle of his trousers.

To her concern she found that a flush of heat seemed to be enveloping her. Pull yourself together, she admonished herself sharply. Luc clearly wasn't embarrassed, so why should *she* be reacting so stupidly?

'Now, roll your weight from one side to the other,' she told him. 'And as you do so, lean forward and gradually tug your trousers off.'

'It's just a little more difficult than you make it sound,' he muttered sardonically as he wrestled with his trousers, fighting to ease them down over his lean hips.

'I'll help you if you like,' she offered.

'And deprive me of a lesson in independence?' he said witheringly, breathing hard as he struggled.

Elise watched as he rolled sideways again. He might be stubborn, she thought, but he certainly had tenacity. Finally, bent almost double, he wrenched his trousers off and tossed them to the end of the bed.

She retrieved them and hung them over the back of a chair before sprinkling some talc on to her palms.

'I'm going to give your legs a quick massage to stimulate the circulation, and then we'll finish off with the passive movements I was telling you about,' she remarked as she returned to his bedside.

'I can hardly wait,' Luc said caustically.

'Were you this appreciative of everything that was done for you in hospital?' she asked, daring to throw a little of his sarcasm back at him.

'You're getting paid, aren't you?' he snarled.

'I don't do my job simply for the pay,' she told him

as, with firm, circular movements, she began to massage his legs from the feet up.

'The halo's very fetching,' he sneered, before snapping, 'How much longer is this going to take?'

'Why?' she asked. 'Do you have something better to do?'

'You're insolent!'

'So are you!'

Her heart fluttered at the threatening scowl Luc gave her. For some reason the live warmth of his hair-roughened skin beneath her palms wasn't helping her to stay in control of her temper. Luc's fierce blue eyes stayed on her as her skilled hands kneaded and relaxed his thigh muscles which had stiffened up while he had been sitting in the wheelchair.

His icy gaze unsettled her and, wanting to break the silence which already seemed oppressive, she remarked, 'I was surprised you didn't seem more interested in what's been going on in the winery while you've been in hospital.'

'As a lesson in living life at second hand, you mean?' he said harshly.

'Is that how you see it?' she asked, glancing up.

'How the hell else do you think I see it?' he snapped with mounting ferocity.

'But that's a ridiculous way of looking at it,' she protested. 'Dr Dercourt believes——'

'I don't want his opinion on everything quoted at me round the clock,' he snarled angrily.

'You're doing it again,' she sighed. 'You're jumping down my throat at my every remark.'

'Then keep your cheery comments to yourself!'

'You seem determined not to like me,' she replied shortly.

'Well, that's something else we can doubtless work on over the next few months,' answered Luc, deftly mocking her clinical manner.

Elise glared at him and for an instant their eyes locked. A strange electricity seemed to flicker along her nerves and, disliking the sensation, she quickly dropped her gaze. Her thoughts were angry and agitated. She simply mustn't let him antagonise her. He was her patient and it was vital to his interests that they work together successfully.

Her voice was pleasant as she said, 'Now we'll start on the passive movements.'

Luc didn't favour her with a reply. His face remained rigid and expressionless as he tolerated the treatment, and she had the strongest impression that he was curbing his frustrated rage with the greatest difficulty.

As she finished, she rubbed her hands together to get rid of the last traces of the talc and said, 'You can take your underpants off now.'

To her relief he accepted her brisk order, merely growling the comment, 'The exercises didn't take long.'

Tactfully she moved away to the chest of drawers to fetch a pair of his pyjamas, keeping her back to him as she said, 'The purpose of them is to take each joint through the full range of its movements. Just over five minutes for both legs is all it takes.'

She turned round to see he had completed undressing. With the muscles bunching in his sinewy arms he hauled himself against the pillows, such power in the movement, it was hard to remember that half his body was paralysed. She noted the gleaming strength of his broad chest, the dark smudge of hair that grew in a line down to his loins, and for an instant her breath seemed to catch in her throat.

'Seen enough?'

The harsh, taunting voice made her start. Feeling hot and more than a little flustered, she went to the bed, where she handed him his pyjamas. The skin at the back of her neck prickled, and, if only because of it, she said clinically, 'You're not a man to me, Monsieur de Rozanieux, merely a case.'

'And when was the last time anyone *was* a man to you, Mademoiselle Sterling?' he jeered, something savage in the taunt despite its softness.

Elise checked herself just in time from telling him it was none of his damned business. Not realising how green and stormy her eyes had become, she said crisply, 'You need to throw your pyjama bottoms down to your feet. Then lean forward and pull them on.'

'It's a wonder the English Health Service could afford to part with you,' he drawled derisively.

She was in no mood to spar with him even in a veiled way when he was still magnificently naked. Quickly she picked up his trousers, which she'd hung over a chair-back, and put them on a hanger in the wardrobe. Perhaps, she thought, as she continued to work with him she would understand how it was he could ruffle her so effortlessly. She just could not seem to help the angry hostility in him striking an answering spark in herself.

Reaching to the top shelf, she fetched two extra pillows.

'What the hell are you doing now?' he demanded curtly.

'These are to support your legs,' she told him as she bolstered the pillows against his calves and ankles. 'Keeping them straight prevents straining of the hips and knees.'

'Is part of the appeal of working with paraplegics that of having the chance to fuss over a man in a nice, cosy, platonic relationship?' asked Luc caustically.

'I can't see our relationship ever being cosy,' she answered shortly.

'Or platonic?'

There was something sensual in his harsh voice, and she rebelled against it as much as if he had touched her. A slight edge of temper showing in her voice, she said, 'Can you raise your weight up for a minute?'

'To submit to still more of your tiresome ministerings?' Luc ground back as he took his weight with his hands.

Elise smoothed the sheet beneath him with a brisk sweep of her palm.

'You may find them tiresome,' she said crisply, 'but they're preferable, I can assure you, to getting bedsores that would hurt your chauvinistic pride as well as your bottom!'

'You're a credit to your profession, Mademoiselle Sterling,' he snarled sarcastically.

She glared at him for an instant. Then, moving to the door, she said, with a calmness that was still intact, if by now totally feigned, 'Your pain-killers are by your bedside if you need them. I hope you sleep well.'

CHAPTER THREE

WHATEVER sort of night Luc had, *she* slept badly. She turned yet again, dragging the pillow more comfortably under her cheek as she tried to relax and drift off. But, instead of being able to, her mind kept replaying the series of sparring matches she'd had with her patient. She knew it was to be expected that she should be the prime target for his savage frustration. His sarcastic comments should have been so much water off a duck's back. So why was she lying awake, annoyed and thinking of all the remarks she would have liked to have made in reply?

She was not smug, annoyingly cheerful, sexually repressed, or any of the other things Luc had mentioned to date. Neither was her job some kind of sublimation for the caring side of her nature. Who exactly did he think he was, anyway, that he could insult her indiscriminately? She couldn't remember ever treating a patient she'd taken to less. Yet the plain fact remained that the onus was on her to try to establish a tolerable relationship between them.

Well, tomorrow was another day, she thought sensibly, before indignation made her flicker her eyes open again. The nerve of the man in accusing her of being solely interested in the impression she was making on Dr Dercourt! No, worse than that, in accusing her of chasing after him!

She turned on her back and lay staring up at the shadowy ceiling. Almost without her realising it her resentment changed slowly into something akin to half-angry defensiveness. She wasn't involved romantically with Dr Dercourt or with any other man, and she didn't mean to be. She was perfectly happy as she was.

Yet she couldn't suppress the sharp ache that surfaced beneath her ribs. With her throat tightening, she curled up into a ball. She didn't want to remember what it was like to feel abandoned and betrayed. But although she was determined not to think of Richard it was a long time before sleep finally came to her.

The autocrat in the wheelchair was not in the dining-room when Elise joined Fabienne and Michel for breakfast.

'Monsieur Luc said he would have a tray in his room,' Brigitte informed them as, having filled the coffee-cups, she set the pot down near to Fabienne.

'Why isn't he having breakfast with us?' asked Michel as the housekeeper went out.

'Because he wants to be by himself, I imagine,' his mother answered, adding, 'Michel, be careful, you're spilling jam on the cloth.'

'I wish Bernard would take me to school in the Land Rover,' Michel declared emphatically. 'It's much more fun than the Mercedes.'

'Is that because you like a bumpy ride?' asked Elise with an amused smile.

Michel nodded, his dark eyes kindling.

'And I like helping Uncle Luc when he goes round the vineyard,' he said brightly.

'If it weren't for the accident, Luc would be out already this morning, checking on the state of things,' Fabienne interposed with a soft sigh.

'It's important because of the frost,' Michel stated, proud to demonstrate his knowledge.

'Because of the *risk* of frost,' Fabienne corrected him, before explaining to Elise, 'With the warm weather there's always the risk at this time of year that the vines will come on too fast and then be damaged later.'

'*Maman*, who's going to pick me up from school?' Michel put in.

'Bernard will.'

'You've changed your mind about going into Montpierre today?' queried Elise.

'To the boutique? Yes, I have. I know what Claude said, but my manageress is very capable, whereas here there's such a lot to do. Next month the trade visitors will be arriving to sample the wines and to decide if they intend to buy. I don't want, when I hand things back to Luc, for them not to be properly in order.'

'When I'm bigger,' Michel said confidently to Elise, 'I'm going to drive one of the harvesting machines. They're huge! I'm going to drive a tractor too. I know where all the controls are already, because sometimes I'm allowed to sit in one.'

'Under strict supervision, and only when it's stationary, I hasten to add,' commented Fabienne with a smile.

'Have *you* ever driven a tractor, Elise?' Michel asked.

'No. You see, I've never lived on a farm. But I can ride a horse.'

'That means you can come with me when I go riding,' Michel said eagerly. 'Have you seen the stables?'

'I wouldn't mind seeing them again when you get home from school,' responded Elise.

There was a tap at the door, and the chauffeur came in.

'*Bonjour*, Bernard,' Fabienne greeted him. '*Comment ça va?*'

'*Très bien, merci, madame.*'

'Are you ready, Michel?'

The little boy nodded, setting his cup down on its

saucer with a slight clatter and getting down from his chair. He submitted to having the traces of a moustache of crumbs wiped from his upper lip by Fabienne before giving her a quick hug and kiss.

As he ran to the uniformed chauffeur, Elise pushed her chair back and said, 'It's time for me to be starting work too.'

There was a note of purpose faintly perceptible in her voice. However scathing and hostile Luc was with her this morning, she had made up her mind she was not going to be provoked in any way by him.

Nikki had nosed his way into his master's room, so that the door stood ajar as she went in. Luc was already up, sitting by the french windows, his eyes fixed broodingly on the sunlit terrace.

His monogrammed dressing-gown looked well on him. Yet not even civilised maroon silk could alter the impression he gave of ferocity and danger, an impression that was somehow heightened by his ruffled hair and dark, unshaven jaw.

Something, Elise assumed it was contempt, flickered in his icy blue eyes as his gaze swung to her. Nikki was lying by the right wheel of his chair, and Luc's hand dropped to stroke the dog's ear. It crossed her mind that, just as centuries of domestication hadn't outbred the resemblance to a wolf in the Alsatian, so Luc's cultivated and aristocratic background seemed not to have tempered in the least his raw, aggressive masculinity.

He raked her from head to foot, his granite-hard face expressionless. She doubted very much that what he saw met with his approval. Her white piqué dress was smart, and she liked the turquoise piping on the collar and elbow-length sleeves. More than that, its simple cut gave her the freedom of movement she needed. Her make-up was skilled, a hint of warm beige on her cheekbones, dusky eyeliner and mascara emphasising her clear green eyes. But with her coppery hair caught up in a topknot, her only jewellery her gold wristwatch, and wearing predominantly white, she supposed that to him her appearance would seem antiseptically clinical.

'It's a lovely morning,' she began with a smile that was intended to disarm him. 'I'll just run your bath for you, and then we'll get started on some exercises.'

'Don't you ever tone down the bright manner?' he said scathingly. 'Or has it just become second nature to you?'

'I could always come in frowning, but I don't expect you'd like that much either,' Elise pointed out calmly.

She noticed the tray that he had set aside on the bedside table, and was glad to see that he hadn't spurned breakfast. It looked a shade precariously balanced and, meaning to push it more securely on to the bedside table, she advanced into the room.

As she did so, the Alsatian rose to his feet. Standing tense in every muscle, he growled at her menacingly. Elise started a little. Not daring to approach any further, she looked at Luc to call the dog off, hating the gleam of scornful amusement she saw in his eyes.

'Outside, Nikki,' he ordered lazily.

The dog obeyed immediately, slinking past her, his tail held low as he padded to the door. Elise's wary gaze followed him out.

'One less snarling brute to have to deal with?' Luc mocked sarcastically.

It was lucky that surprise gave her eyes an expression of innocence and candour, or he would have known how close he'd come to guessing her thoughts. She thought she had been putting up an excellent show of professional pleasantness, and his taunt did not endear him to her. As she moved his breakfast tray to a safer position, she said a shade coolly, 'I'm not frightened of Nikki. But now that he's gone, I'll run your bath.'

'I may be in a wheelchair,' snapped Luc, 'but I'm still capable of turning on the taps!'

Whenever he snapped at her, his voice loaded with such derision, she felt her temper rise in response. Yet outwardly she seemed quite calm and controlled as she said, 'What I'm concerned about is whether you can assess the temperature of the water.'

'*Bon sang!*' he exclaimed with muted fury, his voice rising. 'Do you think I haven't got the sense to try the water with my hand?'

The barrage of his rage made her heart start to thump. Was it some instinct for self-defence that made her want to yell back at him, or did he challenge her in some deeper, inexplicable way? She didn't even think of working out an answer. She was too preoccupied with trying to appear placid and unruffled.

'And what about your balance when you do that?' she asked. 'I don't want you to fall into a bath full of water.'

'Really?' he sneered. 'That surprises me. I should have thought that to humiliate your patients would give you a great feeling of power.'

'And what makes you . . .?' she began with quick anger before hurriedly checking herself. Her eyes still sparked, but she managed to say evenly, 'Please, let's not start the day off snapping at each other. It's not very productive.'

'Not more platitudes,' muttered Luc in contempt.

There didn't seem to be a reply she could make to that without irritating him even more than she seemed to be doing already. In any case, her normally inexhaustible restraint was starting to wear thin already. Annoyed by it, she turned and went into the bathroom.

Was she handling him all wrong? she wondered, feeling uncharacteristically rattled. This morning they were getting on no better than they had yesterday when she had been bold enough to answer him back pretty smartly. Perhaps that was the only technique that would work with him. After all, why expect to keep a snarling brute at bay with smiles and politeness?

He certainly didn't appear to appreciate kindness and care, she thought, then was conscious of a prompt twinge of guilt. The truth was, he stirred in her none of her usual feelings of compassion, and what was so aggravating was that she didn't know why. She was trying to be caring, but it didn't come from the heart as it always had with her other patients. For some strange reason, although he was in a wheelchair, Luc de Rozanieux was a man who defied any feelings of pity.

Elise turned on the bath taps and, noticing the bottle of Paco Rabanne Pour Homme bath essence among his toiletries, she added some of it to the water. Its fragrance was sharp and bracing, and critically she sniffed at the bottle, her nose crinkling. Concentrated, the bath essence was still more pungent and masculine. It was exactly the fragrance that Luc would choose, she thought drily. Everything about the man was too damn dominant!

Returning to the bedroom, she told him, 'Don't dress after you've had your bath. All you'll need is a towel draped round you.'

'You mean you're not coming in to bath me?' he sneered.

'Luckily my thwarted maternal instinct doesn't extend to bathing fully grown men,' she retorted.

Whatever reaction she had been expecting, it certainly wasn't the one she got. His laughter was a surprise. Low and rich, it was every bit as masculine as the rest of him, and Elise caught her lips curving wryly in response. Inadvertently her eyes met his and, as they did so, the mirth in his suddenly died, snuffed out as if it had never existed. A curious tension flickered between them before, with a savage push, Luc propelled himself into the bathroom.

He really was the most incomprehensible man, she thought with a mixture of puzzlement and annoyance as she stared after him. They had been on the point of sharing a joke when, for some reason, he had slashed her again with his icy, contemptuous stare. It seemed like a deliberate slap in the face.

While he was bathing she stripped the bed. She removed the blankets and folded them. Then she replaced the bottom sheet with a fresh one, intending that he would lie on the bed for a back massage. As she worked she listened attentively to the sounds in the bathroom. In some ways Luc's obstinate independence was good, but it had to be set against the risk of his hurting himself.

One of the maids came in for the breakfast tray. Elise handed it to her, seeing as she passed the bathroom door that Luc was now shaving in front of the washbasin.

'Do you mind if I put the radio on?' she asked, thinking that music might cover a hostile silence when he joined her.

'Go ahead.'

The words themselves were friendly enough, even if the tone of voice wasn't. There had to be some way of establishing contact with him. Elise was more than just puzzled by her inability to establish a rapport with him. She was a touch chagrined. Ruefully she realised she'd become rather proud over the years of her ability to get on with her patients, whatever their moods and temperaments.

When Luc returned to the bedroom he was well-shaved and his hair, still wet from the shower, showed the lines of a comb. She watched as though unable to help herself as a drop of water started from one dark strand to trace down the tanned column of his neck. Promptly she recollected herself. She didn't want to admit it, but the fact was he made her nervous.

'Is the pain in your back any easier this morning?' she asked pleasantly.

His eyes narrowed a little, his thick, straight brows coming together above his nose. Why did he have to be so contemptuous of her?

'When did you develop psychic powers?' he asked scathingly.

She knew her next comment wouldn't please him, but there was little point in trying to placate him when every attempt only produced the opposite result. She said, 'Well, something had to be making you so short-tempered last night.'

'Then, in view of the fact that I'm still damned short-tempered this morning,' he growled, 'perhaps you can work out the answer.'

'That's roughly what I thought,' she said. 'So in that case I'll start by giving you a back massage. It should help to relieve the pressure on the nerves.' He didn't move, so she instructed, 'I need you on the bed.'

With any other patient she wouldn't even have realised that her remark held any sexual overtones. But the moment she saw the glitter of harsh amusement in his blue eyes the innuendo struck her. She was glad she didn't colour easily, for there was something faintly insulting about his cynically amused gaze.

'Then turn on to your stomach,' she told him crisply. She paused and asked, 'Are you comfortable?'

'Half my body's paralysed,' he growled in reply. 'How comfortable do you think you can be when your legs feel totally dead?'

'I want you to relax as much as you can,' she said, ignoring his snarled comment.

The muscles of his shoulders bunched as he rested his forearms against the mattress, turning his face against his strong tanned hands. Elise found she was staring at him as he lay naked, apart from the towel over his lean hips, and hurriedly took herself in hand. She'd seen a man's muscular torso and the dark curling hairs on a man's thighs before, hadn't she? And in view of the practice she'd had with massaging patients, there was no reason whatsoever for her to feel the least bit tremulous at the thought of running her hands over the warm, firm contours of his back.

Briskly she sprinkled talc liberally on to her hands. Normally she was good at making small talk with her patients. With Luc she didn't even try. She was concentrating too hard on trying to fight her sexual awareness of him. She slid her palms over his shoulders, identifying each lean, sinewy muscle as her hands roamed lower. Rhomboideus major, Latissimus dorsi . . . Naming the muscles as she worked helped her in her attempt to view him dispassionately, as though he were no different from one of the anatomical drawings of her training days.

She wasn't the only one who slowly began to unwind. Under the firm yet gentle authority of her caressing hands, Luc gave a long, deep groan of satisfaction.

'Oh, that feels good,' he said on a sigh. 'Now I know what Claude meant when he said you had a gift.'

Elise was conscious of an unexpected glow of pleasure. Praise certainly made a welcome change from scathing comments!

'I'm glad it's helping,' she murmured.

'If ever you decide to open a massage parlour,' he said lazily, 'I'll finance you. You'd make a mint!'

'Do you think a massage parlour would go with the brisk hospital manner?' she asked.

The ripple of amusement that went through him travelled into her hands. She smiled, knowing that she was doing her job well, her rhythmic caresses easing the tightness from his muscles. Luc's breathing was deep and steady. He turned his head more comfortably against his hands before asking in a sleepy drawl, 'What made you decide you wanted to be a physiotherapist?'

This made three comments in a row without him snarling at her. It was quite a breakthrough.

'I always knew I wanted to work in a hospital,' she told him. 'I come from quite a medical background. My grandfather was a GP, and so's my father.'

'You mean you're carrying on the family tradition?'

She wasn't sure whether there was an edge of derision in his deep voice, but decided to give him the benefit of the doubt.

'Yes, I suppose I am in some ways,' she agreed. There was a short, surprisingly easy silence, then she remarked, 'I understand from Fabienne that the château and its vineyards have been in your family for three generations.'

'Making me a traditionalist too?'

His face was turned towards her, his eyes closed, his thick lashes dark against his cheek. She caught a glimpse of his lazy smile as he spoke. He definitely wasn't her type, but she had to admit he was attractive in a brutal sort of way, when he wasn't flaying her with his tongue.

'I expect you'll want your son to carry on,' she answered.

Luc's dark head lifted a fraction, his hands balling into fists as he stiffened.

'It would seem that my having a son will depend on you,' he said sarcastically.

Elise's hands stilled.

'I . . . I beg your pardon?' she faltered.

The low sound in his throat was a mixture of mocking amusement and contempt.

'There's no need to get all cold and clinical,' he jeered. 'I'm not about to rape you with the aim of begetting an heir. I was referring to the fact that cripples don't make very good husband material.'

She felt herself colour, and was thankful he couldn't see her face. Just what had she thought he meant? she asked herself crossly. Of course, if he wasn't so aggressively and threateningly male she might not feel quite so defensive, which would help considerably when it came to thinking straight.

'I have every confidence that you'll walk again,' she stated simply.

'Meaning that there's a very fair possibility that I won't,' he reminded her, an edge to his voice.

'A possibility, but Dr Dercourt——'

'Who's never wrong,' he cut in caustically.

'*I've* never known him to be. In fact, I'd back his judgement against anyone's when it comes to diagnosis. And he believes you'll walk again.'

Luc's mouth quirked cynically.

'And if I don't?'

'A lot of patients I've worked with have been happily married with families. Being in a wheelchair doesn't have to preclude that.' Elise paused and then went on, guessing what was on his mind, 'But if what's bothering you is the question of——'

'My virility?' he snapped.

'I know that at present you have no sensation in your legs, but there's no reason——'

'You mean that if a woman has no objection to being made love to by a man whose body is half dead, then there isn't a problem?' Luc cut across her sarcastically.

She moved away from him to sprinkle some more talc on her palms, which were becoming clammy. Heavens, what was wrong with her? She'd reassured patients before about sexual anxieties, so why was she conscious suddenly of a flush of heat enveloping her?

The answer confronted her the moment she turned back and looked at him. The sunlight fell across his near-naked man's body, accentuating the bronzed swarthiness of his skin and the dark hairiness of his arms and legs.

'No woman who loved a man would think of it that way,' she told him.

He propped himself up on one elbow, his jawline tight as his icy gaze impaled her.

'I suppose no amount of self-sacrifice is too great for a woman in love?' he sneered between clenched teeth. 'Not even though it means her own life would be curtailed, that she'd be a virtual prisoner because of her husband's wheelchair?' He snatched hold of her wrist with sudden violence, not seeming to care if he hurt her as he said harshly, 'Your platitudes are endless, but I doubt very much if such an empty existence would be enough for *you*.'

His tanned fingers were biting into her skin, the blaze of anger in his blue eyes sending static flickering along her nerves. The enormity of his barely controlled temper unnerved her. She could feel the force of it like some invisible electricity, an anger that seemed to be directed not at fate but positively at her.

Reacting to his personal attack, she flashed back stormily, 'It would be if I loved you!'

Luc released her contemptuously, his shrewd gaze raking her delicate slightly flushed face and her slim frame.

'You're a liar, *mademoiselle*,' he said with dry derision. 'Despite the prim and proper exterior, I reckon once you'd thawed out you'd give a man a hell of a run for his money. Being tied to a cripple for life wouldn't suit you at all.'

'Well, as the question's hypothetical, I can't see that it matters,' she retorted stormily, 'because first, I'm not going to marry you, and second, I mean to get you out of that wheelchair.'

The clash between them set the tone for the rest of the morning. The exercises, which Luc clearly regarded as a demeaning demonstration of his handicap, made him still more caustic and sarcastic. Finally, refusing to co-operate any longer, he wheeled himself out on to the terrace. Elise glared after him. She hated to be defeated, but the plain fact was that his will was stronger than hers, and it was pointless to exhaust herself any further by arguing, however reasonably, with the raging autocrat. Heels tapping smartly, she walked out of the room.

In the hall she paused, taking a long, calming breath. Perhaps they both needed time to cool off. She'd never met anyone who could ruffle her the way Luc did. Glancing at her wrist, she saw that the red marks had faded, but she knew she would be lucky not to have a bracelet of bruises there tomorrow from the savage brute.

She crossed the hall, deciding that a walk in the grounds might help her to regain her sense of perspective. On the steps she met Bernard.

'I was coming to find you, *mademoiselle*,' he began.

'I forgot to give you the keys to the Renault this morning.'

'The keys to the Renault?' she echoed. 'I'm sorry, I don't understand.'

'Monsieur de Rozanieux said you intended going sightseeing in your time off, so you were to have the use of one of the cars,' Bernard explained.

He walked away, leaving Elise weighing the keys lightly in her hand in totally exasperated perplexity. Her patient was impossible to fathom. She had got him firmly labelled as an impossible tyrant, and now he had to confuse her by thoughtfully putting a car at her disposal!

So what was she supposed to do? She didn't feel very inclined to go back and thank him when she'd just been sworn at so savagely. Not only that, but in his present mood he was likely to snap her head off. Continuing down the steps, she decided to say 'thank you' later.

Her walk took her through the estate's parkland, bringing her back finally along the drive. The château gleamed pearly white, making a striking contrast with the surrounding greenery. Swathed in sunlight, it had almost a hint of fairytale Gothic about it with its high slate roof, pepperpot turrets and dormer and stone mullioned windows. Architecturally intricate and very elegant, an artist's impression of it appeared on every label of the château's wine.

A red Ferrari was parked on the sweep of gravel drive in front of the stately entrance. As Elise strolled towards it, a dark-haired woman in a crisp Chanel suit came out of the house. Her tight, knee-length skirt showed off long legs, while her straight paprika-coloured jacket was unbuttoned and worn with just the right degree of negligent casualness. Her glossy hair was short, with a heavy, cropped fringe. A slim clutch bag in the same tan snake as her high-heeled court shoes was tucked under one arm.

Seeing Elise, she ran lightly down the steps, her gold earrings dancing against her cheeks.

'You must be Luc's physiotherapist,' she began.

Her rush of friendly charm somehow lacked substance. Its insincerity was promptly confirmed by the narrowed measuring-up glance she gave Elise before she continued with a smile that was meant to captivate, 'How do you do? I'm Chantal Charron. I'm sure Luc's told you all about me.'

In fact her patient hadn't once mentioned Chantal, but as tact was necessary Elise said, 'You were with him in the accident.'

Chantal nodded. She plunged her hands into her jacket pockets, hunching her shoulders in a dramatic display of nerviness.

'If it hadn't been for Luc I wouldn't have escaped from the car. I'm sure I don't have to tell you how dreadful all this has been for me. I feel so responsible!'

'It was the drunken driver who was responsible,' Elise said quietly.

'Yes, that's what everyone tells me,' Chantal answered tautly, 'but I can't help how I feel.'

'Monsieur de Rozanieux certainly doesn't blame you, so why blame yourself?'

Chantal nodded, pressing her lips together as though bravely fighting back tears. Then, with a tremulous smile, she said, 'I wish I could be as practical and down-to-earth as you. I wish, too, that Luc wasn't so proud and stubborn. Then we could get married straight away and I could show him how much I love him, that it doesn't matter to me that he's crippled.'

So this elegant woman was Luc's fiancée. Suddenly, for no reason she could think of, Elise found herself being still more critical of Chantal's stagy manner.

'But at the moment Luc doesn't seem to care about anything,' Chantal went on, 'not the vineyard, not the future, not even our marriage. I don't think he can face up to the thought that he may never walk again.'

'He's angry about it,' Elise answered, 'but compared to a lot of people he's facing up to life in a wheelchair with a great deal of grit,'

Chantal seemed not to like the speed with which Elise had leapt to her patient's defence. Her eyes hardened before she curved her mouth into a false smile.

'How are the two of you getting along? I understand from Luc that you had a bit of a brush with him this morning.'

Was she jumping to conclusions, or was Chantal secretly hoping that she and Luc were going to fail to work together successfully? She seemed the possessive type, and it was quite possible that she felt threatened by the closeness implicit in the patient-therapist relationship. Deciding it was best to be open, especially as Chantal's possessiveness could cause complications, Elise said, 'Do you mind if I speak frankly?'

'Please do.'

'You're right, we did have an argument this morning over his treatment, and I don't expect it will be the last. Sometimes therapy can seem almost cruel in the demands it makes on the patient. I know all your instincts must be to want to make it easier for your fiancé. You're bound to feel protective. That's why it's so important that I have your trust and support.'

'You've got both, naturally,' Chantal answered a shade coolly. 'In fact, I hope we're going to be friends.' She put a joke into her voice, but the warning in it remained clear as she added, 'Just so long as you don't fall in love with your patient.'

Score ten out of ten for female intuition, Elise thought. Chantal was jealous of her. Meaning to reassure her and conscious of a stab of pain as she remembered how well she had learned her lesson, she said, 'I find I get very involved with my patients, but I don't fall in love with them.'

'Even in a wheelchair, Luc has all the excitement of a man with a keen, passionate mind. Surely you find him attractive?' probed Chantal.

What Elise found was that he was arrogant, self-willed and even menacing, but she could hardly say as much to his fiancée. Instead she said sympathetically, 'I know it's hard to see someone else caring for the person you love, but——'

'You're not implying I'm jealous, are you?' Chantal cut in haughtily. She threw back her head and burst into unexpected laughter. '*Ça alors*, I believe you are! Listen, Mademoiselle Sterling, I only said what I did out of concern for you. Luc and I are much too close for him to have eyes for another woman, let alone his physiotherapist. But he's extremely charismatic, and I'd hate it if you got hurt.'

Elise knew Chantal meant her derisive words to cut, and was all the more determined to remain indifferent to them. Calmly she said, 'Your warning isn't necessary.'

Chantal studied her with cold, unfriendly eyes.

'Just remember it, that's all,' she snapped, adding coolly, 'I'll see you tonight at dinner.'

She slid behind the wheel of her low-slung sports car and roared off, sending the gravel chips flying. Wondering why she even bothered to try to communicate either with her patient or his theatrical fiancée, Elise turned smartly and went back inside the house.

CHAPTER FOUR

'NOW that you've got the hang of it, I'd like you to try that exercise again, this time on your own.'

As she spoke, Elise retreated a couple of steps to give Luc more space. If her nerves were frayed from being snarled at non-stop for two hours, she didn't show it.

'I thought the aim was to get me out of this damned wheelchair,' growled Luc, the harshness of his voice accentuated by the effort he was expending, 'not to make me some kind of gymnast in it!'

'Patience just isn't your long suit, is it?' she said with light irony.

The comment earned her a savage glance from under lowered brows.

'I think the fact that you're still here after a fortnight's unmitigated misery testifies to the contrary,' he said grimly. 'You were painted by Claude as some kind of miracle worker. I'm still waiting to see the evidence of it.'

'How much progress do you *expect* to make in a fortnight?'

'Is that going to be the same answer I'll get in a month's time, six months' time, a year?'

'Healing's a matter of time.'

'So you keep telling me,' he ground back.

Deciding there was no point in arguing with him, Elise said with professional calmness, 'Will you transfer on to the bed now?'

'Don't you think you've inflicted enough torture on me for one afternoon?' he snarled.

'If I didn't do my job thoroughly, you'd be the first

one to tell me about it,' she began, all ready to say more if Michel hadn't come wandering in through the french windows at that minute.

She felt some of the tension ease in her shoulders as with his entrance the tinder-box atmosphere became slightly less charged.

'What is it, Michel?' asked Luc, his voice still gruff but with a kinder note in it.

'I'm bored,' the little boy sighed. 'When will *Maman* be home?'

'Some time after six,' Luc told him.

'She's never at home any more,' Michel complained as, eyes downcast, he stood fidgeting at the foot of the bed.

'I tell you what,' suggested Elise, 'you go and fetch your remote-control car from your bedroom. By the time you come back I'll have finished giving your uncle his therapy, and you can show me how it works outside on the terrace.'

'For all the good you're doing here, Mademoiselle Sterling, you might as well go now,' Luc observed drily.

'Why do you always call Elise Mademoiselle Sterling?' Michel wanted to know.

The sardonic glance Luc gave her recalled a previous clash of steel striking against stone. With an edge of irony in his voice, too subtle for Michel to catch, he explained, 'Because when a physio is treating a patient, it's what she prefers to be called.'

'Are *you* going to come outside in a minute too?' Michel asked hopefully.

Luc's face became expressionless again as he answered, his intonation faintly self-derisive, 'I have to rest.'

'When you sit still all day, why do you get so tired?'

'It's the muscles in my legs that get tired,' said Luc, the clenched tightness of his jaw at variance with the surprising mildness of his reply.

To put a stop to the little boy's questions, Elise interposed quickly, 'Hurry up, Michel, and fetch your car.'

'OK,' he agreed, diverted, unaware as he scuttled out of the vibrating tension he left behind.

'You're very quiet, *mademoiselle*,' Luc observed sarcastically, his icy gaze sharp and angry. 'I was sure you'd have some comment ready about how hard it is for a child to understand what it's like to be confined to a wheelchair.'

'Michel only wants to have things back the way they were before the accident, with you able to play with him, and his mother home in the evenings.'

'There's no reason why Fabienne shouldn't be home with Michel,' snapped Luc. 'It's up to her if she chooses to put in long hours at the winery instead of working part-time in her boutique.'

'She hasn't much option,' Elise pointed out, 'when every time she consults you about a problem you don't want to know. If only you'd take an interest in the business, Fabienne wouldn't be half so busy. It would be better for her and better for Michel.'

'You mean I should make myself less of a burden,' Luc summarised with growing anger.

'I didn't say that.'

'Or were you thinking that it would give me less time to feel sorry for myself?' Luc continued with his attack.

'Stop putting words into my mouth,' she countered. 'All I'm saying is that it's not impossible to work from a wheel——'

'You know as well as I do that the contribution I could make would be minimal,' Luc interrupted harshly. 'The most I could do would be to see to the accounts. Or was that as much as you were thinking of—a short spell of occupational therapy each day to take my mind off things?'

'Somebody has to do the bookwork.'

Luc regarded her contemptuously. The only indication of his dangerously contained anger was the nerve that jumped in his lean cheek. With an enquiring lift of one dark brow he asked, 'Tell me, are you and Fabienne colluding in this touching little attempt to sustain the illusion that, despite being paralysed, I'm still of some use around here?'

Elise stared back at him, her eyes cool, though her heart was beginning to race nervously with what she was contemplating. A sharp, stinging, below-the-belt remark might just jolt him out of his frustrated bitterness. But did she really dare to say what she had in mind to a man whose anger was already simmering at boiling point?

Tilting her chin, she remarked, her tone every bit as derisive as his, 'You know, it's time you did some thinking, Monsieur de Rozanieux. When you're next brooding on your lot in life, why don't you work out what you want to be—a cripple in a wheelchair, or a man in one?'

Luc's nostrils flared, and she braced herself for the storm force of his temper. It didn't come. She caught her breath in surprise as he leaned back against the pillows and laughed shortly and without mirth. Cynical amusement still in his eyes, he said caustically, 'You're very good at doling out the medicine. Why don't you try taking a little of it yourself for a change?'

'Your sarcasm's wasted on me. I don't know what you're talking about.'

'Then you're more obtuse than I took you for,' he fired back, his voice vibrant with angry scorn. 'You have the gall to suggest I'm acting like a coward when one blow from life has turned you into a clinical iceberg. I don't know what man hurt you in the past, and I don't want to know, but before you start criticising *me*, some self-analysis on your part wouldn't come amiss.'

Elise flinched almost visibly, her eyes darkening. For an instant she felt totally off balance, as groggy with shock and pain as if he had actually struck her. It was the hospital training that stiffened her spine, stopping her from fleeing in tears.

Her voice was tight as she said with the best pretence of cool indifference she could muster, 'I'm sure you've heard the English saying about sticks and stones. That didn't hurt one bit.'

She turned quickly, conscious that it would take only one more caustic comment from him for her poise to splinter. Luc didn't answer her, but she heard his fist strike the mattress with savage frustration as she went out.

Michel's lively chatter as he demonstrated how to bring his remote-control car round in a wide circle on the terrace helped her to stop dwelling on Luc's words. It was after she had gone upstairs and was taking a shower that they came back to her again, producing the same feelings of rawness and anger.

The rose-geranium soap and cascading jets of water for once failed to soothe and revive. How had Luc guessed about her unhappy love affair? Surely it had been a shot in the dark—a painfully accurate one, she thought resentfully. And then she remembered the probe of his hawkishly keen gaze that evening at dinner when she had mentioned her knowledge of wines. A panicky fear stirred in her. Suddenly she found herself actively hating her patient, not just for his arrogant maleness and savage temper, but for seeming to see into her soul, for making her feel defensive and unsafe.

In defiance at being called a clinical iceberg, she paced over to her wardrobe in her lace-trimmed bra and briefs and selected a very feminine flared skirt in navy and indigo which she teamed with a pin-tucked silk blouse. She was extremely glad that Dr Dercourt had asked her to go to the Son et Lumière show at Chenonceaux with him, followed by dinner somewhere. She more than needed a break from her aggressive patient.

The sound of a car drawing up outside interrupted her thoughts. Glancing at her watch, she realised it must be the doctor arriving. However had she been so long changing? Quickly she finished pinning up her hair. She fastened her gold bracelet, sprayed her pulse points with Diorissimo and, picking up her jacket, went downstairs.

'Mademoiselle Sterling! Come here!'

Elise started at the imperious barked summons. She'd already seen that the door to Luc's room stood ajar. If only she could have hurried across the hall silently, but the heels of her bow-backed court shoes on the marble floor made that impossible. From the drawing-room came the muted sound of the doctor's voice as he chatted to Fabienne. Unwillingly, instead of joining them, she changed direction.

Luc was sitting in his wheelchair, his features stern. Pausing just inside the door, Elise began, 'Did you want me?'

She was off duty and, after his words to her earlier, she didn't particularly care that her brisk question implied that he was delaying her.

His gaze raked her from head to foot.

'Am I right in thinking you're going out this evening?' he asked, his tone faintly scathing.

'Yes, you are,' she answered.

Her abruptness did not deter him from probing further, a taunt in his voice, 'You're being very reticent.'

'I'm going to Son et Lumière at Chenonceaux.'

'Who with?' he demanded.

The combination of his implacable personality and her defiance seemed to make the air crackle with electricity. Resenting his interrogation, she retorted crisply, 'Can I remind you that this is my time off? Presumably I *am* allowed out.'

'I said who with?' he insisted.

'Why does it matter who with?' she flashed back, her unwillingness to tell him an answer in itself.

There was a moment's silence while Luc regarded her with derisive diamond-hard eyes. Then he smiled faintly, the vertical grooves down his cheeks deepening with sardonic amusement as he said in a tone that bit with sarcasm, 'So you've finally got a date with Claude. Well, congratulations!'

'You really go out of your way to be unpleasant, don't you?'

'There's no need to be touchy,' he taunted.

'Who wouldn't be, subjected to your constant sarcasm?'

'Tired of playing the saint after only a fortnight?' he asked with mounting ferocity.

Elise's eyes blazed as she fought to master the impulse to retaliate. It was one thing to answer him back occasionally, another to be provoked into a full-scale flaming row. Taking a deep breath, she said with forced calm, 'I don't know why you called me in here, but if you don't need me for anything, Dr Dercourt's waiting.'

'Then don't let me keep you,' snarled Luc.

She walked from the room, adamant that she was not going to let another clash with him ruin her evening.

Dr Dercourt was a comfortable person to be with, and she chatted to him easily as they headed along the main road. In the deepening dusk the poplars along the banks of the Cher seemed almost unnaturally distant. Occasionally she caught a glimpse of the river itself, its surface turned to polished pewter in the waning light.

'Forget your patient for a while,' Dr Dercourt said gently, breaking the thoughtful silence she had lapsed into.

'What?' said Elise, startled, turning her head to glance at him. She gave a rueful laugh. 'I'm sorry—I suppose Monsieur de Rozanieux *is* on my mind. I'm not getting on too well with him at the moment.'

'I guessed as much,' said Claude, his gaze returning to the road. 'When I called round the other day I noticed you were looking rather careworn. Fabienne mentioned this evening that you seem to be taking the brunt of Luc's temper.'

'Was that why you suggested a show and dinner this evening?' Elise asked with a smile.

The doctor quirked an amused brow in her direction.

'I have to admit it did cross my mind that you might be glad of a sounding board. But that aside, I was sure Chenonceaux would appeal to the romantic in you.'

'You don't know how nice it is to be called a romantic,' she said feelingly. '"Antiseptically brisk" is what my patient calls me, among other things.'

Dr Dercourt laughed and swung the Citroën into a space near to where a number of coaches were parked. Already at the start of the season Chenonceaux was drawing large parties of tourists, and there was a steady progression of people up the long, plane-tree-bordered walk to the sphinx-guarded entrance.

Leisurely Elise and Dr Dercourt crossed the moat-enclosed terrace. From there they strolled through the formal gardens which gave perhaps the most arresting view of Chenonceaux. Pale and eerily beautiful in the glow of the floodlights, it stood silhouetted against the darkened countryside, its arches spanning the placid river with all the majestic grace of the Renaissance. Elise halted for a moment simply to stare.

Claude smiled at her reaction.

'It is breathtaking,' he agreed, before asking, 'Did Chantal tell you that the gardens here are being used as the setting for her latest modelling assignment?'

'No, she didn't,' Elise replied, adding, 'but then we rarely talk.'

Claude slanted an enquiring glance at her.

'How's that? I thought Chantal was a frequent visitor, or have things changed between her and Luc since the accident?'

'Not that I'm aware of. No, what I meant is that Chantal isn't especially friendly with me. In fact, I'd no idea she's a model. I assumed she worked on her father's newspaper.'

'He would have liked her to,' Claude answered, 'and for a while her modelling was quite a source of friction between them. He still doesn't really approve of the amount of time she spends in Paris, or the way she's always flying off to different places. If it had been either of his two sons who had gone against his wishes, Jean-Jacques would very quickly have brought him back into line, but Chantal's always been his favourite. Though even she knows not to displease him too much. For instance, even if the accident hadn't happened, she'd have seen she was home for the big celebration the family's planning for her father's sixty-fifth birthday.'

'It must be a double anniversary,' Elise observed. 'I saw in *Le Clairon* that it's also forty years since Monsieur Charron took over the ownership of the paper in Montpierre.'

'Yes, that's why the party's to be on such a grand

scale,' said Claude, teasing her as he added, 'It should give you the chance to see how we French celebrate in style.'

'It won't if Chantal has anything to do with the invitation list,' Elise answered with a touch of humour.

'I wonder if she resents your relationship with Luc,' Claude said thoughtfully. 'Jealousy can prompt some strange behaviour.'

'So I read in the guide-book,' Elise said, determined to keep the conversation light and to forget the problems surrounding her work.

The doctor laughed.

'I see you know how Catherine de Medici had a hole cut in the floor of her study so she could spy on her husband with his mistress in the bedroom below. Yes, that's certainly a case in point.'

These details, together with how Catherine had eventually forced Diane de Poitiers to exchange Chenonceaux for the sterner château of Chaumont, were recounted in the fascinating Son et Lumière. Returning to Montpierre, where Dr Dercourt had booked a table at one of the restaurants in the main square, made a very pleasant way of rounding off the evening.

As they sat over coffee and Cointreau, he remarked, 'You know, we've chatted about a lot of different things this evening, but we've hardly mentioned your patient.'

'It's been more interesting than talking shop,' Elise answered with a smile.

Claude studied her quizzically for an instant. Then he observed meaningfully, 'When someone like you starts mulling over the problems she's encountering instead of talking them out as if it were any other case, I begin to wonder if she mightn't perhaps be getting a little too emotionally involved with her patient.'

'Not a chance,' she assured him.

Claude didn't contradict her, but she had the feeling he wasn't entirely convinced. And, crazy though it was, later she found herself thinking about what he had said.

She most certainly wasn't emotionally involved with Luc, but there was no denying she had strong feelings about him. Was it the situation that was responsible for that, or the man himself? She supposed she simply wasn't used to devoting all her energies to just one patient and, never having lived in before, she found it much harder to switch off in her free time.

The clock in her room showed her that it was almost midnight, yet although it was late she knew she wouldn't sleep if she put the light out immediately. She had too much on her mind. She glanced for her book on the bedside table before remembering that she had left it in the drawing-room.

Should she go downstairs and fetch it? There was no doubt she would cope better with another demanding day if she'd enjoyed a good night's sleep. Her pale green wrap was lying near the foot of the bed. Putting it on, she left her room, tying the sash as she went quietly downstairs, careful not to disturb the somnolent silence.

She had reached the bottom step when she heard a noise. She froze in the silvered moonlight, her heartbeat quickening. Not sure what it was she had heard, she listened carefully in the stillness that was dense and absolute. And then the sound came again, from Luc's room. He seemed to be groaning. Elise's heart skipped a beat with the fear that he had fallen. Without her to support him, perhaps he couldn't get up.

She sped across the hall in her green satin mules and hurried into his room, not sure whether he was calling out weakly for help or moaning in pain. There was a lamp on the bureau immediately inside the door, and she hurriedly switched it on. In its soft glow she could see Luc lying in bed, the sheets tangled roughly round his hips, his swarthiness emphasised by their whiteness.

Her relief that she hadn't found him sprawled on the floor was promptly replaced by a different concern as she saw the sweat that glistened on his face and the feverish way his head twisted from side to side. His voice was choked but clearly audible as he implored angrily, 'Move . . . Stand clear . . . For heaven's sake, *someone* . . . get her out of the way!'

The anguish that cramped his voice appalled her. For an instant it seemed as if she was transfixed to the spot by the intensity of his frustration and torment. It didn't seem possible that the man who lay moaning, almost sobbing, his chest gleaming with sweat as he twisted and writhed, was the mocking, sarcastic patient she knew, who was always so eternally sure of himself.

Luc had seemed the last person on earth ever to need consoling or comforting. Never until tonight had Elise once seen him vulnerable. For the first time it wasn't the physio in her that made her rush to his side, but a genuine and devastating compassion. Leaning over him, she put a gentle hand on his bare shoulder.

'Monsieur de Rozanieux——' she began in a throaty whisper.

But the hold of the nightmare was too strong for her voice to reach him. He muttered again, his face distorted with pain, his dark head still wrenching from side to side on the pillow. She sat on the bed as this time she shook his shoulder insistently.

'Monsieur de Rozanieux! Luc, wake up! Everything's all right—it's just a dream.'

His inky lashes flickered before his eyes opened suddenly to stare at her with such blazing blue intensity that she started a little.

'Elise . . .?' His voice was dry and hoarse as he sat up with a leashed energy that suggested he was still in the iron grip of the nightmare. He grabbed hold of her by the arms before the return of consciousness made him blink and he released her. Still sounding a shade hoarse, he demanded, 'What are you doing here?'

'You were having a nightmare,' Elise explained, her own voice huskier than usual. 'Don't you remember? I was coming downstairs to fetch a book when I heard you call out.'

He nodded slowly, running a hand through his hair, disarraying the black strands even further. When his eyes returned to her again he was in total command of himself.

'What do you want a book for at this time of night?' he asked with a touch of dry humour before saying, 'Go back to bed now. I'm fine.'

'No, you're not,' she contradicted him. 'The sheets are all wrinkled and the covers are in a tangle. Get up and I'll remake the bed for you.'

'It's all right as it——'

'It will only take me a minute,' she interrupted with quiet firmness. Then, suspecting he was sleeping nude, she added quickly, glad that in the soft lighting, even if she were blushing, he wouldn't see it, 'I'll pass you your dressing-gown.'

'Thank you, *mademoiselle*.'

He sounded amused by her. Was there no fathoming the man? Only minutes ago he had been reliving the car crash with harrowing vividness. The images must still be chasing through his mind, yet here he was almost teasing her for fussing over him. Hiding her puzzlement, she stripped the bed, remaking it with neat hospital corners.

The glow from the lamp illuminated her face softly as she worked, turning her auburn hair that fell loosely over her shoulders into a fierier red. She picked up the pillow and, still trying to work him out, she glanced at where Luc was sitting in the wheelchair.

As she had sensed, he was watching her with those mesmerisingly blue eyes. The night and the quietness of the rest of the house somehow created a disturbing aura of intimacy, and static seemed to flicker along her nerves, making her feel defensive with him even before he asked, 'How was your evening?'

Her arms went round the pillow, hugging it to her waist as though it were a shield against what she took to be subtle but malevolent sarcasm. Meaning to lay the topic to rest once and for all, she said with an imperceptible tilt to her chin, 'How many times do I have to tell you? I am *not* chasing——'

'I know you're not.'

For an instant, surprise robbed her of an answer. Then, remembering Luc's repeated accusations, she said a shade heatedly, 'Well, if you knew——'

'Simmer down,' he growled. 'I'm not getting at you. What I'm trying to do is to apologise.'

'For saying . . .?' she faltered, so staggered by his change of attitude towards her that she didn't know quite how to react.

'For everything,' he muttered wearily as he rubbed the back of his neck. He sighed, the tension and bitterness mysteriously vanished from his manner, subjecting her to the full force of his masculine charisma. 'You've been patience itself this last fortnight, and all I've done is snarl at you. I meant to apologise to you earlier, before you went out.

Instead, having called you into my room, I was my usual unreasonable self.'

Still holding the pillow, Elise perched on the bed so that she was sitting opposite him. She stared at him, not answering but noting his dark, lightning-bolt eyebrows, the aggressive thrust of his jaw, the uncompromising yet sensual mouth. The gap between the lapels of his robe revealed the swarthy column of his throat and the mat of dark hair on his chest.

It was because there was something so indomitable and animal and dangerous about him that she had found him impossible to pity. So why was it that suddenly those very same qualities should make her rebel against the injustice of fate that had him crippled in a wheelchair? And here he was apologising to her, giving her an accolade for the care she had shown him when not once till now had it been prompted by anything more than professionalism.

'Well, say something,' growled Luc.

Elise bit her lip, guilt making her voice a little throaty.

'I . . . I was thinking that at times I've been rather clinically brisk with you. I should have been . . . warmer.'

Luc's mouth twisted bitterly.

'It wasn't you I was angry with when I lashed out at you this afternoon,' he said. 'It was myself—not that it's any damned excuse for saying something I knew would hurt you.'

She averted her eyes, unwilling to meet his astute gaze. He was much too perceptive, and it frightened her to feel exposed. Giving the pillow a brisk pat, she leaned towards the head of the bed to return it to its place, saying as she did so, 'It's forgotten.'

Luc studied her an instant before saying, 'You

know your trouble? You're too controlled. You never let the lid off your feelings. Maybe if you stopped keeping them so tightly in rein, you'd get him out of your system.'

Her heart began to race in alarm. She couldn't be this transparent, so how had he managed to discover so much about her in so little time? Could he see everything that went on behind her façade of poise? she wondered in a panic.

She forced herself to look at him and then to laugh naturally. 'What *him*?'

Luc's steel-blue eyes narrowed, his eyes impaling her as he said calmly, 'As a liar, you're quite convincing.'

Elise stiffened, her gaze becoming cool and hostile. Six years had passed since Richard had broken off their engagement on the eve of their wedding. It was to have been a big occasion in the small Oxfordshire village she came from, with everyone wanting to give a good send-off to the daughter of the popular local GP.

She remembered the hurried cancelling of the arrangements, the returning of the presents that should have graced her new home, the kindly meant yet wounding words of consolation from family and friends. A kind of numbness had helped her to get through the day that should have been her wedding day. The sharp rise of pain and misery had come later.

'Even if someone did hurt me once, I've come to terms with it,' she told him, hearing the tightness in her voice that betrayed her.

'Sure you have.'

'I *have*,' she insisted.

She would have surged to her feet, but Luc caught hold of her by the wrist. To try to free herself would mean a tussle. Her only hope in her battle for calm was not to engage in a physical struggle with him that she was bound to lose.

'It often helps to talk,' Luc said quietly.

Unable to trust her voice, Elise couldn't even snap at him defiantly that she wasn't in need of comforting. In any case, it blatantly wasn't true. In the silence Luc's hand slipped over her wrist to enclose her fingers. His warm clasp was reassuring, and yet it sent a strange flicker of electricity along her nerves.

After a moment she capitulated in a cramped voice, 'I . . . I was jilted, but it was a long time ago and I'm over it now.'

'What happened?' he asked gently.

She looked down and then, without knowing how it was, found herself admitting in a husky whisper,

'It was the day before my wedding. My fiancé told me he was in love with someone else and wanted to marry her.'

'Who was the someone else? Someone you knew?' Elise bit her lip and shook her head.

'She . . . she was the chairman's daughter of the wine company he worked for. Richard never said so, but she sounded far more sophisticated and glamorous than I am.'

'Don't sell yourself short. You're both those things, and more.'

She was surprised by Luc's quiet forcefulness. She could sense his eyes on her, but couldn't raise her own, and he went on, 'It sounds to me as if your fiancé had an eye to the main chance. Have you never thought that perhaps you had a lucky escape?'

'Richard wasn't like that!'

'No, of course not,' he agreed drily.

'He wasn't! He loved Suzanne. He——'

Her voice caught and she broke off. It hurt far too much for her to be able to recount how Richard had told her that it was meeting Suzanne that had made him realise that all he felt for Elise was affection and tenderness. He'd confused feelings of gratitude for the care she'd shown him during his stay in hospital with love. He knew he should have told her before, but he hadn't been able to find the courage.

'He what?' Luc prompted.

She shook her head. Suddenly she wished she hadn't admitted so much. It was only the compulsion of his personality that had forced the confession out of her. She felt his thumb move caressingly against her palm, and a hot little shiver seemed to run over her skin.

She glanced up at him, her eyes very bright. They were completely alone together, she was far too conscious of him as a man, and talking about the past had made her dangerously vulnerable.

Quickly she withdrew her hand and got to her feet. Conscious of a desperate need to return to a more clinical and safe relationship with him, she said in a rush, 'But it's you we should be talking about, not me. If your sleep pattern's disturbed with nightmares, you may need a short course of sleeping tablets.'

Kindly he pretended not to see that she was very close to tears.

'I'm on quite enough medication with painkillers, thank you,' he said with dry humour, adding, 'And in any case, as you undoubtedly know, tablets aren't the cure for everything.'

After their conversation of a few minutes ago Elise couldn't fail to catch his implication, but he made no further reference to what she had told him as she made sure that he was comfortable for the night.

Yet his remark made her thoughtful. She went back to bed wishing that she did know the cure for heartbreak. She wished, too, that she could help Luc make more progress. He maddened her and he was forever shouting at her, but tonight she had seen a glimpse of him as he must have been before the accident had left him paralysed. She realised that beneath the frustration and the bitterness there was a man she liked very much.

CHAPTER FIVE

ELISE woke later than usual the next morning. Michel had already left for school, and only Luc and Fabienne were at the breakfast table. Her patient glanced up as she joined them.

'I thought you'd be tired after last night,' he began. 'I wasn't expecting to see you before nine.'

When he wasn't snapping at her, Luc's voice had a husky quality she found attractive, disturbingly so. His steel-blue eyes sent a familiar flicker of static along her nerves, but she held his gaze, finding for the first time that it no longer required an effort of will to do so. Last night had altered their relationship, and even if she'd had the least inclination to, she couldn't have put the distance back between them.

'Were you hoping to escape a session of therapy?' she asked, daring to tease him.

Her humour wasn't wasted. Luc's tone was sardonic as he answered, 'No. I've already realised that, results or no results, the treatment goes on.'

'What did you think of Chenonceaux, Elise?' Fabienne interposed, as though afraid the conversation was on dangerous ground.

'It's certainly whetted my appetite for more sightseeing!' answered Elise, sipping her coffee.

'Why don't you plan a trip to Blois?' Fabienne suggested. 'It's only about thirty kilometres from here and it's full of history.' Pushing back her chair, she went on, 'I'm sorry I've got to rush off, but I've a hectic day ahead. I'll see you both later.'

'There's no need for you to go into the winery this morning,' Luc told her with a frown.

Fabienne's shoulders tensed.

'Luc, please,' she said tautly, 'let's not get into this argument again.'

'I meant that from today I intend taking over from you,' he said, as though the matter was settled.

Elise was every bit as surprised by his statement as his sister. Till now Luc had shown an attitude of total indifference towards anything related to the business.

'What's made you change your mind?' Fabienne asked with a bewildered little laugh as Brigitte came in with more hot croissants.

For an instant a dark brow was slanted at Elise.

'Being in a wheelchair doesn't mean I have to act like a cripple,' he said drily. Addressing his next comment directly to her, he went on, 'I take it my therapy can be fitted in so that it doesn't clash with work.'

Having gained her confirmation, he turned his head to speak to Brigitte.

'Tell Bernard I'd like the car round at the front in ten minutes, would you?'

Elise had assumed he intended summoning the bailiff to the house. She supposed she should have known better. It was because Luc was a man of action that he made such a difficult patient. Having decided to resume control of the business, he wasn't going to be satisfied with relying on other people's reports. Concerned about him, and thinking that if she was with him she could at least stop him doing too much, she said quickly, 'If you're going in to the winery this morning, I think it might be better if I drove you, just so that I'm on hand.'

'Are you afraid to let me out of your sight?'

His voice was mocking, but he wasn't being scathing, merely ribbing her with his sarcasm. If it hadn't been for last night, she doubted she would have recognised the subtle difference.

'I thought you liked having me within earshot,' she answered innocently, and marvelled that his mouth actually quirked with wry amusement.

She drove the Renault, as she was used to it and the wheelchair fitted without difficulty into the boot. It wasn't far to the winery. The road climbed steadily uphill, the chalky soil encroaching on to its margins and the rows of leafy vines stretching away in neat order on either side. In the distance the Cher glinted in the gentle sunlight, its surface reflecting like some ever-changing mirror the greenery of its banks and the faintly cloud-swept sky.

Luc didn't seem particularly inclined to talk, and after several moments of silence, broken only by the hum of the engine, Elise darted a glance at him, trying to guess his mood. He was gazing thoughtfully at the landscape, the strength of character in his face even more evident in profile. She wondered whether the vineyard was on his mind, or whether perhaps the nightmare still haunted his thoughts.

Almost against her will she remembered the desire she'd felt last night to put her arms around him, to dispel the torment of his dream with her body's warmth. In the light of day it seemed an extreme reaction, and her pulse quickened merely with the thought of it. Yet the wish to offer comfort in some form was still there. She would have encouraged him to talk about the nightmare at the time if their conversation hadn't taken such a wayward turn. As she hadn't, she said now, 'You don't seem any the worse for last night. The nightmare you had couldn't have kept you awake.'

'I don't need a lot of sleep, which is just as well if you plan to make a practice of slipping into my room in a diaphanous robe on the stroke of midnight!'

It was the word 'diaphanous' that robbed her of an

articulate reply. Luc's faintly amused masculine gaze stayed on her as he remarked, adding to her embarrassment, 'There's no need to go all quiet and stiff merely because I've reminded you you're a woman.'

Elise decided against dignifying his taunt by rising to it. Conscious that her skin felt hot, she asked, hoping her voice sounded as calmly pitched as usual, 'What was your nightmare about?' Luc laughed at her brisk change of topic, and she said in swift self-defence, 'There *was* a purpose to the question. It's not at all uncommon for a harrowing experience to cause recurrent nightmares, and I was——'

'You're a walking medical encyclopaedia,' he drawled, cutting across her as he looked out at the rolling farmland.

'You wouldn't be human if the crash wasn't still very vivid in your mind.'

Her comment brought his gaze back to her. His brows drawn together, he said, 'If you're thinking the nightmare I had was about the crash, it wasn't.'

'Then what . . .?' she began, before realising she was wrong to take his denial at face value. She hadn't misheard his tortured mutterings. Quietly she said, 'You know, having a nightmare isn't some sign of weakness. There's no need to feel ashamed——'

'Do you ever let a subject drop?' he growled.

'Are *you* ever going to let me finish a sentence?'

'I might, if you'd stop quoting amateur psychology at me,' he answered.

'It's not amateur psychology, but a plain fact that the subconscious gets to work on anxieties and memories the waking mind keeps suppressed. Bottling things up never helped anyone.'

'Are you speaking from personal experience?'

Elise flashed him a glance, knowing only too well what he was referring to, but declined to answer.

'You know, you're a fine one,' Luc commented. 'You hand out the most practical advice, but you never think to heed one word of it when it comes to your own life.'

Keeping her gaze on the road, she said, 'Do you mind if we change the subject?'

'Have you ever talked about your broken engagement properly with anyone?' he asked.

'I'm well past the stage of needing a shoulder to cry on,' she told him as casually as she could, very glad to see the winery looming up ahead of them.

'Has there been anyone else since your fiancé?'

'I don't see that that's any of your business, any more than your engagement to Mademoiselle Charron is any affair of mine.'

Her defensive comment earned her a threatening look from under sharply drawn together brows.

'Who the hell told you I'm engaged to Chantal?' demanded Luc.

'She did,' Elise answered. 'I know it's unofficial, so there's no need to snarl at me. I'm not going to be tactless and repeat it to anyone else, if that's what you're thinking.'

'You'd better not!' he shot back.

His cease-fire certainly hadn't lasted long! she thought wryly as she let Nikki out of the back of the Renault. The sun was warm on her bare arms and softly enhanced the whiteness of the winery that was built into the limestone cliff. Geraniums grew in urns on the low wall that ran alongside where the car was parked.

Elise opened the boot, pausing for an instant to look out over the vineyard which stretched away in the clear light with all the pristine freshness of a watercolour.

'Are you going to take all day?' Luc called out gruffly.

Sometimes she wondered how he'd managed before he'd had her to order around!

'I didn't know you were timing me,' she answered.

'Since you've been here, you've become damned quick at answering back,' he said, but despite his growl she caught the faint note of amusement in his voice.

She lined the wheelchair up, unable to hide a smile as she replied, 'I've learned that I have to be, to hold my own with you.'

Luc hauled himself into the wheelchair and as he did so Henri Bassac, one of the admin staff, came out of the office building, his eyes on the papers he was checking against his clipboard. As he glanced up, his face broke into a wrinkled smile. He hurried over to them, clasping Luc by the hand with typical French effusiveness as he began, 'It's really good to see you, *monsieur*. The place hasn't been the same without you.'

'It's good to be back,' Luc answered with a laugh. 'How is everything here?'

'There have been one or two problems which I expect your sister's told you about, but luckily nothing major's cropped up while you've been away.'

As he finished speaking he gave a nod of acknowledgement to Elise, which seemed to remind Luc of her presence.

'Henri, is there someone free at the moment who could give Mademoiselle Sterling a tour of the cellars while she's here?' he asked.

'I'll find someone right away,' Henri answered. 'Will you come this way, *mademoiselle*?'

'You'd better get your jacket from the car,' Luc told her. 'It's cold in the cellars.'

He could make even a casual comment sound like a directive, Elise thought without rancour as she reached across the back seat. After one of the hardest two weeks she'd ever had with a patient, suddenly a bridge of rapport seemed to exist between them.

She didn't especially want to dwell on the way Luc had held her hand while she had told him about her broken engagement. It evoked feelings that she found disturbing, but she was still strangely touched by the kindness he had shown her. Last night they had both seemed to discover that the other was human. Certainly she would never think of him again as an irascible tyrant.

She shrugged on her jacket, her eyes straying in his direction. With Nikki pacing obediently at his side, he was propelling himself towards the office. His dark hair glistened in the sunlight, and she could see the power in his broad shoulders. Flinty determination seemed stamped in every line of him as he pushed with an easy rhythm at the wheels.

Henri followed her gaze before commenting, respect in his voice, *'C'est un brave homme, celui-là, n'est-ce pas?'*

'Yes, he is,' she agreed quietly.

Julien, a stocky man in his late fifties, showed her around. Wearing a large white bibbed apron over his trousers, and with a cloth cap on his head, he was a chatty and informative guide.

'There are two million bottles stored here and twelve kilometres of cellars,' he told her, joking as he added, 'But don't worry, we're not going to walk the whole length of them!'

Elise listened to him as they walked along one of the dim main galleries, only occasionally asking a question as she gazed about her, intrigued by the rows and rows of dusty bottles that were stacked against the cold limestone walls. The naked bulbs spaced at wide intervals on the low ceiling made their shadows creep up stealthily behind them out of the gloom and then bound ahead as they approached the next light.

'The bottles stay on their sides here for up to five years,' Julien told her. 'That's why the basic wine we use has to be of such a high quality. There's so much time and skill involved in the champagne process of producing a sparkling wine that dud results would be a disaster.'

Their footsteps echoed as they walked on, the bottles that rested undisturbed in the gloom producing a feeling of timelessness. At the opening of yet another shadowy passage, Julien paused to point out one of the cellar workers who stood with his back to them in front of a large wooden rack.

'The second fermentation of the wine causes a deposit to form. That's why to remove it the bottles are placed in those racks you can see. Every day over several months an expert, like Marcel, turns each bottle, gradually increasing the tilt of it. Then the neck of the bottle is frozen so that a block of ice forms containing the deposit. When the cork is removed the ice shoots out. The space is filled up with sugar syrup, though how much sugar is added depends on the sparkling wine, whether it's to be *brut*, *sec*, or *demi-sec*.'

'How long has Monsieur de Rozanieux been in charge here?' Elise asked.

'He came into his inheritance when he was twenty-one. Of course, thirteen years ago the place wasn't like it is today. It had been neglected and there was no end of work to be done.'

'Why was that?' she asked.

'The estate had been held in trust for over ten years,' Julien told her. 'You see, Monsieur de Rozanieux's parents died when he was only a boy, and he and his sister were brought up by an uncle who owned a farm in Bordeaux. That's why, although Monsieur de Rozanieux has a degree in chemistry, there's nothing he doesn't know about the land.'

They returned along the murky galleries, where the temperature never rose above ten degrees centigrade, to the formal tasting-room. Glasses were set out in profusion for the professional visitors, and the staff were kept busy. Elise thanked Julien for the tour and wandered outside with a glass of *demi-sec*. After the chilly cellars the sun seemed to be shining with dazzling brilliance, and she sat down on the stone wall, enjoying the lazy warmth.

Nikki was lying in a patch of shade, and after a moment he paced over to her, dropping to his haunches not far from her feet. His ears pricked up as she spoke to him, but she checked the impulse to reach out and pat him. Like his master, he might finally have accepted her, but she intended to tread a little cautiously with him.

Luc's mood varied over the next two weeks. Elise refrained from telling him not to take on too much at the winery. With his physiotherapy failing to yield results, she was only too relieved that his work seemed to stop him from brooding over it.

She was becoming uneasy that he still had no feeling of any kind in his legs. Though she kept it to herself, it was a bad sign. After a month of intensive treatment, some sensation should have returned.

Bernard drove Luc to the winery each day now, leaving Elise with much of the morning free. Knowing she must not allow herself to get depressed, she decided to drive into Montpierre. With its smart main shopping street and riverside gardens, it was an attractive town. Having gone to the post office to post a letter home, she strolled to the café near the old bridge. Its terrace was shaded by plane tress, and she sat down at one of the outdoor tables and ordered a coffee.

On the far bank some men were fishing, their lines trailing in the shallows. The graceful arches of the bridge were reflected in the placidly flowing water and even the noise of the traffic sounded remote.

Absently Elise toyed with the wrapped cubes of sugar on the table. She had known from the beginning that Luc's recovery depended on the extent of damage to the nerves in his spine. She had accepted that there was an outside chance of treatment being ineffective, but it had not played on her mind the way it was playing now.

The thought that Luc might remain in a wheelchair for life was insupportable. Fate just could not be that cruel. With a faint sigh she realised that Dr Dercourt had been right. She *was* becoming too involved with this case, far too involved. Yet how could she help it when watching Luc battle with the limitations of his disability only increased her determination to get him to walk again?

She took a sip of coffee and discovered that she had been so deep in thought she'd let it go cold. Paying her bill, she walked back to her car. She must keep her anxieties in check. Her job was to encourage her patient and not to recognise defeat until it was positively staring her in the face. And luckily, she reminded herself, things were not yet at that stage.

She got behind a tractor soon after leaving Montpierre and, unable to pass it on the narrow country road, she resigned herself to a slow drive back. She glanced at her watch, seeing that she had heaps of time to be changed and ready to give Luc his therapy when he returned to the château.

Entering the house, she saw that the double doors to the drawing-room were open, but she didn't think to glance in their direction as she crossed the hall.

'Where the hell have you been?'

The harsh, accusing male voice stopped her in her tracks. She swung round to see Luc, a wintry hardness in his face as he sat with his wheelchair blocking the doorway to the drawing-room.

His awesome and unpredictable temper was hard on her nerves, even without the added strain she had been under for the last fortnight. Dr Dercourt was calling later in the day to give him a routine check-up. Until she could share her fears with him, she bore the burden alone of wondering whether it was becoming a very real possibility that Luc would always be paralysed.

His clenched jaw emphasised the sternness of his features. Elise felt impaled by his narrowed icy gaze, and with false composure answered, 'I didn't expect you to be back from the winery yet.'

'That's abundantly obvious,' he snapped caustically. 'I've been waiting for you so we could get started for the last half-hour.'

'How was I supposed to know you'd want your therapy at a different time today?' she defended herself, conscious of a stab of pain in her temples as she flinched inwardly at his ferocious attack. 'I'm not a mind-reader!'

'So you thought you'd just breeze off,' he summarised angrily.

'Well, why not?' she asked. 'Our session doesn't usually begin until——'

'Our session starts when I tell you,' he cut in, the ring of steel to his voice. 'I employ you as a physiotherapist, not to go touring the whole damn region at my expense!'

'That's not fair!' Elise retaliated, stung by his accusation. 'I went into Montpierre this morning because there seemed no reason why I shouldn't. But till today I've always been on hand the moment you needed me.'

'Tell me,' he jeered, a savage note to his voice, 'has your enthusiasm for the treatment worn off, now that results are starting to seem less and less likely?'

'Of course not!' she answered, a protesting ring to her voice.

Luc gave a grim laugh.

'So,' he said drily, 'you finally admit that we're getting nowhere.'

'No!' she declared. 'Stop twisting what I'm saying.'

'You mean we're to just soldier on,' he jeered. 'You pretend to me that we're actually getting somewhere, while I'm equally polite and pretend we are too. But in the meantime, to make the whole charade a little less tiresome, we skip the odd session of therapy here and there.'

His cutting sarcasm was all the harder to endure because of her own doubts, doubts that as a physio she mustn't heed. She had to have enough faith and optimism for both of them.

'I've already told you,' she said evenly, 'I had no intention of skipping this morning's session. You were back earlier than I expected. And as far as your progress is concerned——'

'Progress?' he interrupted harshly. 'That word's a joke! It implies improvement, in case you hadn't realised it. So far there hasn't been any.'

'That's not true and you know it,' she insisted. 'When you first came out of hospital you had to rely on my help for all sorts of things. Now——'

'I'm a veritable athlete in a wheelchair,' he interrupted again, a glint of cynical humour in his steel-blue eyes.

Elise stared back at him, her mouth set obstinately. It wasn't that she didn't understand how he felt. She understood his frustration only too well, and the bitter resignation in his voice made her heart ache for him. But, determined to be positive, she persisted, 'You seem to forget that what you've accomplished in that wheelchair is an achievement in itself.'

'Maybe it is from where you're standing,' he answered gratingly, giving deliberate emphasis to the final word.

'I'm doing my best,' she flashed back, and was immediately horrified by the tremor in her voice. Steadying her tone, she managed to add, 'And I intend going on doing that.'

But there was no placating him. Instead her words had the opposite effect from the one she had intended. His mouth thinned to a hard line and anger blazed in his eyes. She was all the more shaken by the force of his fury because she had no idea why it was focused so savagely on her.

As so often happened, his temper inevitably struck sparks off her own, yet for once she was almost glad of it. Resentment eased the ache of compassion that had tightened around her ribs. If she were to reason him out of his bitterness, she couldn't afford to feel so much empathy with him.

Throwing out her hands palm uppermost, she asked with curbed exasperation, '*Now* what have I said?'

A nerve jumped along his lean jaw as he answered her in a low, furious tone, the rage that burned in him becoming more evident with each brutally delivered word.

'I've put up with as much pity all round as I can take. The only person I didn't get it from was you. So don't you ever damn well speak to me again with that tender-hearted catch in your voice, not unless you want me to choke it out of you!'

'I don't feel pity for you. Not the way you think,'

Elise denied strongly. 'I'm just sorry that a car crash had put you in a wheelchair, the way anyone with any feelings would be. But regret and pity are two different emotions.'

'Then it's a distinction I can't see,' Luc retorted in a voice that bit with derision.

'You're too proud to see it, that's your trouble.'

Luc's mouth kindled with a cynical sneer. His hands that gripped the armrests with such punishing force relaxed a little, and she should have known to brace herself for his stinging sarcasm as he changed his tactics of attack.

'When you started to thaw out with me,' he commented, 'I didn't realise that I was to be subjected to your cloying sympathy!'

His words cut as they were intended to do, and there was more than an edge of anger in her voice as she protested, 'I can't do anything to please you, can I? First you were always jeering at me for being cold and clinical. Now that I'm warmer with you, you find me cloying. Just what have you got against me that I'm forever in the wrong?'

'Why don't you cry about it on Claude's shoulder this afternoon?' he suggested contemptuously.

His gibe was too much for her.

'Not that accusation again!' she exclaimed, so that for the first time they were both shouting at each other. 'You *know* I'm not interested in Dr Dercourt—not that it's any business of yours! For heaven's sake, what's making you so thoroughly unreasonable?'

'How about that I object to being treated like some juvenile who's got to be shielded from the truth?' he exploded. 'If the treatment's a failure, and I'm going to be paralysed for life, I'd like to hear you say it!'

Elise stared at him. The fear that Luc was never going to walk again had been in her mind for the last fortnight, but to hear it put so savagely into words left her temporarily stunned. But it took her no more than an instant to rally. She would no more allow him to give up hope than she would allow herself to. Her heart was thudding from their heated exchange. Even her breathing was quickened, but her voice rang with conviction as she insisted, 'Therapy doesn't produce instant results. It's still too soon to make any kind of judgement about whether or not you'll always be paralysed.'

'So we keep on persevering,' Luc mocked harshly.

'Yes!'

'For how long?'

'For as long as it takes,' she retorted.

Turning abruptly, she walked towards the staircase, determined to put an end to an angry argument that was going to get them nowhere. She could feel Luc's look of contemptuous scorn between her shoulder-blades, and she expected that at any moment he would roar at her to come back, but the command didn't come.

Having gained the haven of her room, she sank down on the bed. The pain in her temples had magnified into a throbbing headache. It was all very well for her to try constantly to be positive, but how much hope was it justifiable to keep offering so that her patient didn't lose heart? This wasn't the first case to raise difficult issues of this kind, but she had never found it so hard before to find an answer she could believe in.

Determinedly she pulled herself together and started to change. Luc might be a realist, but he was a fighter too. He needed her stubborn optimism. Yet the interrupting thought was that maybe in their close and intense relationship he needed honesty from her even more.

Apart from the occasional curt comment, Luc

scarcely spoke to her during their session together. Once or twice she ventured a remark, hoping he would take her up on it, but though his replies were civil enough they were brusque, giving her the impression that his thoughts were elsewhere.

As the session ended, Brigitte tapped lightly at the door to say, 'Mademoiselle Charron is here to see you, Monsieur Luc.'

'Tell her I'll be with her straight away,' he answered, firing a clipped question at Elise, 'I take it that we're through for the morning?'

She nodded, and his hands dropped to the wheels of his chair, spinning it round expertly with the minimum of effort. As he propelled himself towards the door, she said on the spur of the moment, 'Luc . . .'

He halted, turning the chair back so that he faced her.

'Yes?'

His tone was impassive, his thundering fury long since spent. In some ways she found his grim stoicism even harder to witness than his anger. It was hard to begin, but since he wasn't a man to tolerate tentativeness she plunged in boldly. 'I . . . I understand you're disappointed with the results to date, and . . . and I'd be lying if I didn't tell you I've been a little disappointed too.'

He kept his hard, impersonal gaze on her, no sarcasm in his voice, only a cynical dryness as he commented, 'Well, it's nice to get some honesty from you for a change.'

Determined to strike the right balance with what she said, she hurried on, 'I know you hate it when you think I'm being brisk and cheerful, but although this last fortnight's been hard on you, when Dr Dercourt calls to give you your check-up——'

'He'll doubtless be as good as you are at telling me

that, whatever the evidence to the contrary, I'll walk again,' Luc interrupted harshly, firing his next question at her. 'What lines do you actually draw in the medical profession when it comes to deluding the patient?'

Elise turned with the pretence of smoothing the covers of the bed. Somehow it was easier to keep her voice steady when she didn't have to see his disgust with her.

'All right,' she conceded, 'the outlook isn't as good as I'd like. If I say anything, I expect you'll accuse me of fobbing you off with platitudes, but what alternative is there but to go on trying? You knew when I came here that I couldn't wave a magic wand and have you on your feet again in a matter of days.'

He didn't answer, and she went on, 'It's always hard living on hope—I'm not going to deny that. But can't you see that to stop fighting isn't going to achieve anything?'

He still didn't answer and, exasperated by his lack even of a contemptuous reply, she swung round to face him. What she saw made the words she'd been about to say die on her lips.

Luc was running his palms down the length of his right thigh, his dark brows drawn together in an intent frown. She froze, hoping so desperately for a miracle that she didn't dare ask the question.

And then his eyes lifted suddenly to hers, the blaze of jubilation in them so intense that she managed to breathe huskily, 'Luc, what is it?'

'There's some feeling in my legs,' he answered, his voice a hoarse whisper, gaining in strength as he repeated triumphantly, 'Elise, there's some feeling back in my legs!'

She moved impetuously towards him before a sob from the doorway checked her. Chantal was standing gripping the doorjamb as though without it she would collapse, her face drained of all colour as she looked at Luc.

'Darling?' she whispered tightly. 'Darling, is it true?'

He held out his hand to her and she ran blindly towards him, collapsing at his feet, sobbing incoherently as she buried her face in his lap.

'Don't *mon ange*,' he soothed huskily. 'Don't cry. It's all right—everything's going to be all right.'

Elise looked at Chantal's dark head resting on Luc's knees, looked at the way his strong hands were stroking her hair with such gentleness it made her throat ache. Suddenly she was no longer a participant, but an intruder on a moment of intimate joy between a man and a woman.

They were so absorbed in each other that she might not have existed. The french windows were ajar on to the terrace, and she escaped through them. To anyone watching her from the house she would have seemed quite calm as she approached the stone balustrade. But the hands that she spread out on the warm stone were trembling. A tear ran down her cheek and, bewildered, she realised she was crying, crying with relief for a miracle she had begun to despair of, crying when she had not cried for six years.

Hurriedly she brushed the tears away, trying to recollect herself. In her heart were joy and thankfulness. Yet if she admitted it there was a fierce ache there too, an ache she despised because it was prompted by the image of Chantal at Luc's feet, her dark head on his knees. Selfishly she had wanted it to be only the two of them who had shared the miraculous moment together.

CHAPTER SIX

THE DAY was hot and tranquil, and Elise was half tempted to enjoy a swim until Luc should join her for his hydro-therapy session—the tantalisingly blue pool shimmered and glinted, its surface invitingly smooth. But she resisted the impulse to stroll to the tiled edge and to dive cleanly in. Even for someone as fit as she was, hydro-therapy was fatiguing, and she intended to conserve her energy exclusively for her patient.

She was wearing her regulation swimsuit. In plain navy Lycra, it showed off her trim figure, emphasising the youthful line of her bust and revealing long slim legs. Though she also owned a very pretty flamingo-print bikini, to date she hadn't worn it. Luc made her much too aware of her femininity as it was, without her putting any more of her body on show than was necessary.

Her towelling jacket was hung over the back of one of the wrought-iron chairs, and her wristwatch was lying on the table beside it. She debated getting up from her sunlounger to check the time once more, then abandoned the idea. If Luc had kept her waiting because of a business matter she wouldn't have been put out, so there was no need to feel faintly irritated because Chantal had dropped by and was delaying the start of their session.

The lavish sunlight gave an almost Impressionistic quality to the vista of lawns and gardens, and Elise put her hands up under her head. The sunlight was warm on her bare skin and she relaxed, letting her thoughts drift.

It was the sharp tap of high heels that made her open her eyes. She glanced up to see Chantal coming down the steps from the terrace. In waisted charmeuse trousers and a sleeveless top she managed to look casual and yet glamorous. Skirting the pool, she drew out one of the white chairs from round the table so she could sit down next to Elise, who, on the much lower sunlounger, immediately felt at a disadvantage.

'Luc will be with you in a few minutes,' Chantal told her, commenting with a disapproving laugh, 'Really, anyone would think you were on holiday, stretched out here in the sun!'

It nettled Elise to be criticised for relaxing when it was because of Chantal that she was still waiting for her patient. But, refraining from pointing the fact out, she merely commented, 'It's very restful here by the pool.'

Chantal contemplated her haughtily, and in instinctive defence Elise ran a smoothing hand up to her topknot to check that no silky wisps had come loose. As she did so her fingers brushed an earring, making it dance against her cheek.

With a patronising smile Chantal asked, 'Are you so pleased with Luc's present that even in the pool you can't bear to take your earrings off?'

He had given them to her three weeks ago, soon after he had first regained some sensation in his legs. Patients often expressed appreciation with a gift of chocolates or flowers. But though Elise had been most touched by Luc's thanks, his present had taken her completely by surprise. Opening the small box he'd handed to her, she had exclaimed, 'They're lovely! But, Luc, I can't possibly accept them—they're too expensive.'

'I'd no idea English puritanism went so deep,' he had commented, amused. 'I'm not out to buy your favours, if that's what's on your mind. I merely wanted to give you something lasting as a token of gratitude. If ever I walk again, it will be because of you.'

Answering Chantal's question, Elise said, 'I'd forgotten I was wearing them.'

'What a pity Luc didn't get me to choose them for you,' Chantal commented. 'I'm surprised he didn't realise that the ones he's picked out aren't at all right for your personality. The very ordinary button studs are much more your style.'

'Perhaps Luc sees me differently from the way you do,' answered Elise, feeling she had put up with enough barbed remarks without retaliating.

'Or perhaps you'd like to think he does,' Chantal flashed back.

'I'm afraid I don't follow you.'

'I would have thought my meaning was obvious, but since it suits you to act obtuse, I'll explain. You'd like him to be in love with you, wouldn't you?'

'Oh, don't be so ridiculous!' Elise protested.

'I gave you some advice when you first came here,' Chantal swept on coldly. 'Evidently you've forgotten it, so I'll remind you again. The only reason Luc seems to have any time for you is because at the moment you're helping him. But once you're no longer needed he'll be as ready to say goodbye to you as I shall be.'

Chantal would have said more, but at that moment Luc came out on to the terrace in his wheelchair. Immediately she got to her feet. Putting a hand to her long beads to stop them from swinging, she ran gracefully towards him to take hold of the handles of his wheelchair.

Elise knew that had *she* flown to assist him she would have been promptly roared at. Able now to drag himself along with the aid of a Zimmer frame,

Luc was way past the stage when he needed any help on a ramp with his wheelchair. But Chantal didn't even attract a sardonic comment from him by hurrying to his aid.

For some reason it made Elise feel mutinous, which annoyed her even more. She was his physio, that was all, no matter how intricate and involved their relationship. It was only natural that he treated her differently from the way he treated the woman he was going to marry.

Chantal pushed him close to the table and then returned to her chair. Reaching out to lay a slim hand on his arm, she remarked, 'It's so wonderful, the progress you're making. I was saying to Elise that soon she'll be able to get back to the hospital work she likes so much.'

Elise, irritated at yet another veiled broadside from Chantal, caught the frown Luc slanted in her direction.

'I understood that it would be at least three months before I no longer need any form of therapy,' he said, his hard gaze narrowing on her.

'Yes, that's——'

'You mean you're finding that the routine with just one patient to care for is growing tedious?' he cut in, an edge of sarcasm to his mockery.

Between his temper and Chantal's contriving comments, there was little chance of that!

'I'm not hankering after hospital life, if that's your implication,' Elise told him.

Chantal, pleased with the friction she had sparked so effortlessly between them, turned to Elise to remark with synthetic sympathy, 'You're bound to be a little homesick. But still, next week you'll have a compatriot to keep you company.'

'I'm entertaining one of the buyers from Britain,' Luc explained curtly.

His brusque tone nettled Elise. He was often more curt with her than he was with anyone else. She saw that his jawline was tight and there was a suggestion of anger restrained with difficulty in his eyes. Why his temper was so unpredictable she didn't know, but she was beginning to think she would enjoy the placid company of a fellow Briton for a change.

'What's the buyer's name?' she asked.

'Kempson.'

Her startled eyes darkened as she held Luc's gaze. Hurriedly she looked away, not wanting him to see how shaken she was. Her heart was beating erratically and her mouth suddenly felt dry.

She was jumping to conclusions, she told herself in a panic. Richard couldn't be coming to stay at the château! It wasn't possible. And yet who else could it be, with the name of Kempson?

Chantal stood up, smiling lazily at Luc as she said, 'I must be going. I'd join you for a swim, but I don't expect Elise would approve of my distracting you.' Bending to kiss him, she murmured caressingly, 'I'll see you this evening. Ciao.'

She strolled away from the pool, and Elise, wondering how she was going to bear the pain of seeing Richard again said, her voice a shade tight, 'Are you ready for us to begin?'

Luc studied her consideringly, his steel-blue eyes as keen as a hawk's.

'What was your fiancé's surname?' he probed.

'What do you mean?' she demanded, jolted by his question and feeling suddenly vulnerable and far too easy to read.

'Don't play games with me,' he ordered quietly. 'I didn't imagine the stunned look you gave me when I mentioned Richard Kempson's name, and it's just occurred to me that you said your fiancé worked in the wine trade.'

Elise knew it was going to be enough of an ordeal meeting Richard again, without her perceptive patient guessing everything that was whirling about in her mind. Forcing herself to rally despite her dismay, she said, keeping her voice brisk and steady, 'Yes, I should think it's him. Now, can we get started?'

Luc kept his hard gaze on her a moment longer before shrugging off his towelling robe. He was wearing black swimming-trunks, the animal power of his physique making her for some reason feel even more antagonistic towards him. His body was swarthy and aggressively male, and she found the tangle of black hair on his chest and forearms every bit as shocking as she had when she'd first seen him stripped almost two months ago.

'Well,' he commented drily, 'it will be interesting to see how you and your ex get on together after all this time.'

The faint jeer in his tone shattered her pretence of stoical calm.

'*Interesting*?' she flashed back. 'Do you think I'm going to find it *interesting* to meet up with my ex-fiancé? Or do you mean you're going to find it entertaining watching my discomfiture?'

His dark brows came together in a frown, but his voice remained even and remarkably patient as he said, 'Mr Kempson doesn't have to stay here. If the thought of seeing him again upsets you this much, I'll make arrangements for him to stay at one of the hotels in Montpierre.'

He so rarely bothered to curb his annoyance in her presence that his forbearance made her suddenly conscious of the inexplicable amount of static in the air between them. The desire to yell at him, to relieve her pent-up emotions and at the same time shatter the tension in the storm of an argument, was so fierce in her and so completely out of character that she was alarmed by it.

'I'm not upset,' she told him, struggling to master her feelings. 'And I've no objection whatsoever to Richard staying here. In case you've forgotten, I've had six years to get over him.'

'You mean six years to moon over him,' he corrected.

She had never felt such an urge to slap him.

'Think what you like!' she almost snapped.

'What I'd like,' answered Luc with an edge of sarcasm, 'is to have my therapy, if you can get your mind focused on it instead of your erstwhile lover.'

Elise got to her feet, meaning haughtily to ignore the gibe. Instead the words came unbidden.

'You know, you've really got a nerve,' she said. He slanted a threatening look at her, but she went on, 'You keep me waiting roughly half an hour because you're with Chantal, and then you make out that I'm keeping you waiting!'

'You're supposed to be available when I want you,' he answered, the way his eyes dropped to the length of her bare legs and then travelled up to the swell of her breasts before finally returning icily to her face, making the comment seem deliberately insulting.

A surge of anger quickened her breathing. How she had ever felt close enough to him to confess about her broken engagement she couldn't imagine! She must have been crazy to have deluded herself into thinking that over the last few weeks a rapport had developed between them. Right now she was back to feeling about him exactly as she had done when she'd first arrived at the château.

Putting coolness into her voice, she said, 'Well, I'm available now.'

A gleam of cynical amusement came into his eyes at the way she had dealt with his innuendo, but, walking ahead of him to the tiled edge, she didn't give him the chance to comment on it.

He needed only the minimum of assistance from her now to lower himself into the pool. Usually there was quite a lot of banter and laughter in their sessions. Today there was none. Her instructions were brisk as she went through a range of exercises with him that were to strengthen the arm and shoulder muscles he would need for crutch walking when he progressed to that stage.

He had just completed some circulation exercises when he turned to the rail to push the float he'd been working with on to the tiles with a gesture of impatience.

'Look, let's call a truce, shall we?' he said, running a hand through his wet hair.

'I wasn't aware there was a war on,' Elise answered coldly.

'For heaven's sake, don't be so damned self-righteous!'

'If you want a truce between us, don't snarl at me!'

Luc drew a short breath of exasperation.

'I'll never know why I let you get me so riled,' he said drily.

'It could be that you're plain short-tempered,' she suggested with some of the sarcasm she had learned from him.

His masculine mouth quirked with amusement.

'While you, despite your red hair, are a model of restraint, I suppose,' he returned mockingly.

Because of Richard, Elise was in a stubborn, angry mood. She didn't feel like making up with Luc when he was so obviously laughing at her. But, since further hostility wasn't going to make her feel any better either, reluctantly she forgave him.

'Are you ready to practise the swung-through gait we tried yesterday?' she asked, her tone more conciliatory as she shaded her eyes against the sun's brightness.

'I didn't realise hydro-therapy was going to be such hard work,' he commented, a wry smile deepening the attractive grooves in his cheeks.

Elise tried to ignore the strange way her heart fluttered as she took hold of him by the pelvis, while he placed his tanned, capable hands on her bare shoulders. The fact that she was steadying him didn't alter the effect his nearness had on her, and her pulse felt the strain of trying to remain indifferent to the impact of his masculinity.

The water that lapped her shoulders reached his upper chest, and the top of her head was roughly level with the line of his jaw. Darting a glance at him, she saw his lips compress with the sheer effort it required for him to drag one foot ahead of the other. Her body was braced to take his weight as, walking backwards, she matched his steps. To look up at him would mean establishing eye contact between them at dangerously close range, and out of some instinct for self-preservation she found herself addressing her instructions to the swarthy column of his throat.

'For someone so slightly built, you're surprisingly strong,' Luc observed as she felt her back graze the tiles.

With relief she realised that they had crossed the width of the pool. Meaning to ask lightly whether he meant his remark as a compliment or an insult, she allowed her gaze to meet his.

But instead, as she met the startling blueness of his eyes, her breath seemed to catch in her throat. She was suddenly conscious that, though her own hands had fallen away from him, his still rested on her shoulders, his palms warm and firm on her skin.

His bare muscular chest was only inches away. He had only to bend his head for his lips to graze hers, and the thought alone made her legs go weak.

'You're trembling,' murmured Luc, his voice curiously throaty.

'Even in the pool I find you quite a weight,' she said a shade breathlessly. 'Holding you tires me.'

'It's even more tiring to be supported, believe me,' he said harshly, adding, his tone clipped, 'Is that it for today?'

'Finish off with a couple of lengths of back crawl and then, yes, we'll call it a day,' she agreed, thankful to withdraw from his embrace as he took hold of the rail.

Elise sat on the tiles while he swam. The water's buoyancy gave him a raw, athletic grace that was denied him on land. She noted the gleaming power of his broad shoulders and the way the water, sparkling in the sunlight, flew from his sinewy, backward-flung arms. Watching him expend some of his aggressive male energy as he completed the two lengths made her understand the frustration he must feel walking with a frame.

Reaching the rail, he shook the water out of his eyes. Then, with his palms placed flat on the tiled edge, he hauled himself out of the pool. Elise joined him as, still sitting on the edge, he shrugged on his robe. It was part of her training to be close at hand as he twisted into his wheelchair. The fall in blood pressure caused by coming out of the water meant that occasionally a patient felt giddy or faint for a few minutes, and was glad of a supporting grip.

Pleased with their work in the pool, she told him, 'A couple more weeks and I should think you'll be ready to walk with crutches.'

Most patients appreciated a few words of encouragement, and of late Luc hadn't been so touchy about them, but today his mouth thinned grimly.

'I'm well aware of the progress I've made,' he said, rubbing a hand along the side of his thigh as though he could somehow force strength back into his legs, 'but there's one hell of a way to go yet before I no longer move like a cripple. I want you to get me walking with crutches sooner than in a couple of weeks.'

'If that's a request for more strenuous therapy, the answer's no,' she said firmly. 'You're already in danger of pushing yourself too hard.'

'You're employed to do what I tell you,' Luc said ominously.

'I'm *employed* to give you the best treatment,' she reminded him.

She could hazard a very good guess at what was making him impatient with his progress. Chantal had been scattering charm all over him this morning, but because he was so stubborn he wouldn't marry her until he considered he was no longer a cripple. That was why he wanted the healing process accelerated. Elise didn't know why the thought should aggravate her, but she went on quite shortly, 'So stop ordering me about in your usual high-handed way. You'll walk with crutches when *I* think you're ready, not when *you* think you are!'

'I wonder what's making you so prickly this morning,' he jeered, fixing her with his hard, blue eyes.

She stared at him coldly, just simmering for a good row, but refusing for reasons of professionalism to let him goad her into one. Taking hold of the handles of his wheelchair, she said, forcing herself to stay calm, 'When you've rested, I'll give you a back massage.'

'I will not be treated like some bloody invalid by you!' roared Luc in a sudden explosion of bad temper. 'I don't need you to push me indoors, or to hold my hand while I take a shower. How many times do I have to spell it out to you?'

She let go of the handles, glaring at his back but saying nothing as he propelled himself towards the house. Marching round to the other side of the pool, she gathered up the accessory apparatus she had used with him in their session together. Her eyes were smarting and her throat felt tight, and what was so maddening was that she didn't know whether she wanted to rage at him or simply to burst into tears.

She sat down on one of the white chairs, fighting to get her emotions back in check. Normally in the twenty minutes before she gave Luc his massage she showered and changed, but today she stayed by the pool. She didn't know how she was going to survive the ordeal of next week, but it made no sense for her to add to her problems by getting into a blazing row with her patient.

Though it was the prospect of seeing Richard again that had upset her, strangely it was Luc who dominated her thoughts as she tried to pull herself together. They had been getting on so well of late, and she was completely at a loss to understand what had started him firing sarcastic comments at her this morning, or what had put him in such a bad mood.

She touched the back of her head to see how wet her hair was. Her chignon was dishevelled from the pool, the tendrils that had escaped curling wispily against her neck. But there wasn't time for her to tidy it properly. If she kept her irascible patient waiting, doubtless he would remark on it. Yet, despite her determination not to flare up with Luc again, her eyes were still a shade stormy as she crossed the terrace.

He seemed to have forgotten the way he had shouted at her, and she was only too glad to call a cease-fire. A slight breeze stirred the flimsy net curtains at the french windows that stood ajar. The sunlight that came into the room in a broad parallelogram glistened on Luc's dark head, which rested on his arms.

The conversation between them gave no indication of tension as Elise massaged his shoulders with knowing hands. But as always it required the sternest effort of will for her to ignore the virility that was stamped in every line of his hard man's body.

As soon as he could walk unaided it would be Chantal's long, supple fingers that moved caressingly over his bronzed skin. The thought didn't please her. In fact, there was a tight little ache beneath her ribs.

'You always use talc on your hands,' Luc murmured lazily as she picked up the container to sprinkle some more on to her palms. 'Why not oil?'

'Baby talc is better,' she told him. 'It's not perfumed so it doesn't cause irritation and, unlike oil, it isn't messy. Warm, sticky skin-to-skin contact isn't particularly therapeutic or enjoyable.'

Luc raised his head to look at her, his gaze taking in her slim figure in the navy swimsuit.

'Is that your experience?' he said slowly, and without a flicker of mockery. 'I would have thought your fiancé would have taught you that such skin-to-skin contact can be very pleasurable indeed.'

For an instant she stared at him, his effrontery robbing her of the power of speech. She could feel herself blushing with a heat that wasn't caused entirely by outrage, though it was temper that trembled in her voice as she said, 'I'll thank you to leave the topic of my fiancé alone.'

Luc propped himself up on one elbow. She could sense his impatience with her, but his voice was as steady as his gaze.

'Don't you think that at turned twenty-seven it's time you came to terms with the past? If you fall in love you know you can get hurt, but there isn't a game in the world you can play without the risk of collecting some bruises. That's what makes life a challenge. But you're supposed to learn from the past and go on. Instead you're throwing yourself away because you had the misfortune to pick the wrong man.'

'He wasn't the wrong man,' she flashed back. 'And how dare you imply that all I do is mull over the past? I have learned from it and gone on. I've got a job I like and——'

'And you think that's enough for you?' he broke in.

'Yes, believe it or not!'

'Who do you think you're fooling? You may present a cool, calm front to everyone, but that isn't the real you. The real you is a woman with fire and spirit, and a temper to boot when you let your hair down.'

Her eyes sparked, but her determination to keep in control of herself was equal to her anger.

'If you've no further comments to make on my character, I'd like to continue with the treatment,' she said.

'You mean anything to evade the issue,' said Luc as he rested his head back on his hands. His tone was kinder as he went on, 'Wake up, Elise. Richard wasn't the right man for you when you were engaged. He was a social climber then and not worthy of you, and I'd be most surprised if time's improved him.'

'Whatever he's like now,' she said tightly, 'it's immaterial. He's married and that's an end to it.'

'And of course you wouldn't make a play for a married man,' he fired back sardonically, 'though it doesn't stop you dreaming about him.'

Her right hand rhythmically moulding his lower back seemed to have a temper of its own. It yearned to curl itself into a fist and to thump him.

'I said I'd like you to leave the topic alone,' she said coolly.

'When are you going to realise that a man who dumps his fiancée because a better spec comes along isn't worth loving?'

The urge in her hand grew beyond control. Deep massage could be painful, and she saw from the deliberate twinge she gave him that it was.

He stiffened, his hand shooting out to grasp her wrist. As he turned on his side, his steel-blue eyes impaled her. The tension that had been simmering between them ever since he had joined her at the poolside for the start of their session flared now to flash-point.

He sat up slowly, his grip still holding her prisoner, his voice deceptively mild as he said, 'You little sadist.'

'You deserved it,' she stormed, 'so let go!'

'If you want to yell at me, OK, you go right ahead and do it,' he said, his tone still mild, though his face was as hard as a fist. 'A good yell might be just what you need. But don't you bottle up your temper till it comes out in petty viciousness.'

His words shamed her, making her lash out defiantly, 'If you're expecting an apology, you're not getting one!'

Catching hold of her other hand, he pulled her nearer and swung her on to the bed. She landed diagonally across it, so stupefied by his rough action that for an instant she simply lay where he had thrown her.

Outraged, she glared up at him, her fierce words of indignation fading as she saw the anger that glittered in his eyes. A twinge of fear went through her, and she went to scramble off the bed and out of his reach, but his grip tightened on her wrists as, leaning forward over her, he thrust her arms up over her head.

She gave a little cry of distress before, trembling with fury, she ground out, 'Luc, get off me!'

He didn't answer. Instead, pinioning both her wrists with one hand, he started to take the pins out of her hair.

'What do you think you're doing?' she breathed.

'How long have you lived in that shell of ice?' he asked mockingly. 'Because maybe it's time someone shattered it.'

Their eyes met, a flush of heat enveloping her. She had never found it such a struggle to breathe. She wanted to fight him, but she felt as though she was being submerged, thrust deep into uncharted waters that would claim her soul completely if she didn't find the power to resist with all her might.

She heard her frightened whimper as she tried to shrink away from him. Her hands curled into helpless fists as his strong, swarthy face came closer, and in desperation she turned her head away, exposing the lovely line of her neck and shoulders to him.

His naked chest moved in a caress against her breasts, brushing her taut nipples. An agonising dart of pleasure went through her and, with a sob threatening to choke her, she squeezed her eyes tightly shut, holding herself rigid for the inevitable. She felt the rasp of his shaved jaw against her skin . . .

And the next moment she was free. Luc was breathing every bit as heavily as she, but his hands relaxed. Drawing her up off the bed, he taunted softly, 'Yes, you need to be kissed, my frustrated little vixen. But don't worry, I'm not about to molest you.'

Elise's eyes blazed in her white face as she stumbled to her feet. The frighteningly erotic feelings he had aroused in her only added to her wild fury. Raising her hand, she struck him across the cheek, using such force that his head jerked sideways.

She heard his hiss of indrawn breath. Her fingers marked his tanned skin with white that slowly turned to red. For a cold instant she thought he was going to hit her in retaliation. His jaw flexed and rage burned in his gaze.

She took a step back, her hand covering her mouth to stifle a sob. Turning blindly, she ran to the door.

'Elise, come back here!' Luc shouted.

His furious command didn't even make her falter. Nothing would have made her stop, she was so upset. She fled up the stairs, racing to the safety of her room. Slamming the door behind her, she leaned against it, trembling from head to foot.

Whatever the provocation, however savagely he had treated her or humiliated her, the horrifying fact was, she had struck a patient. She covered her face with her hands, her shoulders shaking.

Still in a state of shock, she went over to the writing bureau by the window. Sitting down at it, she pulled a piece of paper towards her and, forcing her trembling hand to hold the pen, began to write her letter of resignation.

CHAPTER SEVEN

LUC wasted no time in summoning her. The phone by her bedside rang while she was still sitting at the bureau. Pressing the knuckles of her left hand against her trembling lips, she went on writing, too upset to answer it.

Yet the persistence of the ringing made it increasingly hard to ignore and, as she sensed Luc's anger, a feeling of hurt mutiny began to rise up inside her. Suddenly she threw down her ballpoint and glared at the phone as though she were glaring at him.

The ringing finally stopped, and she turned back to her desk, dropping her head in her hands. Another tear spilled into her palm and ran down her wrist. Stubbornly she wiped it away before picking up her pen again.

A few minutes later Brigitte tapped at her door to say, 'Monsieur Luc would like to speak to you in his room.'

Despite the housekeeper's tactful phrasing, Elise guessed it was an order she was relaying, not a request. Forcing her voice past the constriction in her throat, she answered, 'Tell him I won't be long. I want to change first.'

'He said you were to come downstairs at once.'

No doubt to roar at her that he intended reporting her to Dr Dercourt and that she was fired. Only he didn't need to fire her, because her letter of resignation was in her hand. It would have given her more dignity if she had been granted time to slip on a dress and neaten her hair, but his authority was such that she didn't dare defy him.

Thrusting her hand deep into the pockets of her beach jacket, she followed Brigitte downstairs. She felt as if she was still trembling, but her shoulders were squared as she paused for an instant outside Luc's room. Her hand clenched nervously. Raising it, she knocked briskly and walked in without waiting for permission to enter.

He was standing by the window, supported by his walking-frame. The moment she saw him the words she had prepared went out of her head and she said instinctively, 'Hydro-therapy is tiring and you should be resting. Why don't you ever listen to me?'

He considered her stonily, his blue eyes with a chilly glint. His tanned cheek still faintly showed the mark where she had hit him and, seeing it, Elise caught the edge of her lip between her teeth.

'I didn't call you down here because I wanted a lecture on the importance of rest,' he snapped.

She felt defensive and hurt and much too close to tears to argue with him. Struggling to keep her voice steady, she answered quietly, 'I know you didn't. So I'd better give you this.'

The silence seemed menacing as he ripped open the envelope one-handed and unfolded the letter. He scanned the contents briefly, his gaze searing her with its contempt as he glanced up.

'You hypocritical coward!' he said in a voice that bit with derision. 'You learn that your ex-fiancé will be staying here, and before the morning's out you hand in your notice with some trumped-up pretext of unprofessional conduct!'

For an instant his accusation left her stunned. Then, her green eyes blazing with indignation, she began, 'How *dare* you call me a hypocrite and a coward? Richard has nothing to do with my resignation. I'm resigning because I slapped you. I had never slapped anyone in my whole life until——'

'Then you shouldn't have left it so late,' Luc cut across her, 'because your half-hearted fiancé more than gave you reason to.'

'You leave Richard out of this!'

'The letter you've just handed me makes that rather difficult,' he ground back sarcastically.

'Can't you understand?' she stormed. 'My decision has nothing to do with Richard. Do you honestly think I can go on working here after what's happened? Ever since I arrived you've taken a malevolent pleasure in tormenting me, knowing that I couldn't retaliate on your level. Except this morning I *did* hit back, and now I'll never be able to forget that once I slapped one of my patients.'

Instead of answering, he tore the letter in two in a gesture of angry impatience, so that she demanded in confusion, 'What are you doing?'

'I'm not accepting your resignation,' he retorted, his voice as hard as his eyes. 'I told you when you came here that you don't quit until I fire you, and I've no intention of losing a first-class physio simply because she can't get her private life sorted out.'

Infuriated, Elise paced to the foot of the bed, where she exclaimed, 'Talking to you is a waste of breath! You haven't listened to a word I've said, have you? You've no idea how ashamed I feel and how angry . . . Heaven knows why I've stayed here this long when you're so impossible.'

'Perhaps until I mentioned Mr Kempson this morning you'd have considered it unprofessional to walk off a case,' Luc suggested sarcastically.

The well-aimed shot hit home. Elise glared at him, hating him at that moment with every cell in her body.

'All right,' she breathed angrily, 'you win! I won't resign, and I'll go on treating you, if only to prove to you that I'm not running away from Richard. But don't you ever, ever maul me or manhandle me again—holding me down on the bed as if I was to be taught a lesson. You behaved like an animal!'

Luc's mouth thinned. Though he didn't raise his voice, there was a steel-like force behind his words that was every bit as intimidating.

'Because I realise the strain you're under, I'll let that statement go. But unless you really want something to act indignantly over, you won't make the mistake of slapping me twice.'

Her eyes remained rebellious, but she didn't risk answering him back. Instead, as he had made it clear that she was now free to go, she left the room in silence. Yet, although the question of her resignation had been dealt with, there had never been such a yawning gulf between them.

It was one that remained unbridged. Over the next few days Luc directed none of his usual sarcastic comments at her, but his eyes were icy and derisive whenever their gazes clashed. In turn, Elise forced herself to be distantly polite. Their conversations remained coldly fixed on the therapy he was receiving and impersonal topics. Part of her still felt angry and defiant with him for provoking her to flash-point; another part regretted that there was no longer any joking or spontaneity between them.

Richard was due to arrive on Tuesday afternoon and, as the time drew nearer, she began to wish she *had* given in her notice. When six years ago he had broken off their engagement she had never expected to see him again.

She didn't know whether Luc's invitation included both him and his wife, but she was certain she couldn't meet Suzanne for the first time without jealousy burning into her like a brand. Though she could have asked Luc about Suzanne, she didn't.

He'd made too many scathing comments about her feelings for her ex-fiancé. She wasn't giving him the chance to make more.

Dreading the inevitable meeting, she chose to delay it as long as possible. Luc was out for lunch that day and, feeling taut and on edge, she was glad of it. He was far too perceptive.

The sunlight was bright on the terrace and the surrounding garden was a mass of colour. From the gusto with which Michel was clearing his plate, the main course of chicken with mushroom sauce was delicious. To Elise, the meal might have been made of sawdust, and her lack of appetite made Fabienne ask, 'Are you finding it too warm in the sun?'

'No, it's lovely out here. It's just that I'm not very hungry,' she answered. Determined not to let the strain she was under become obvious, she quickly changed the subject. 'By the way, Fabienne, I've been meaning to ask, have you anything in stock that's not too expensive which might suit me for Saturday? I've decided to splash out on something new for Monsieur Charron's party.'

'I've got a couple of very stylish evening dresses in the sale,' Fabienne told her. 'Why don't you come into Montpierre with me this afternoon? You could try them on or see if anything else on the rail catches your eye.'

'But, *Maman*, you promised to come fishing with me,' Michel grumbled.

'I said I'd try to. But as I've got one of the reps coming into the boutique we'll have to go fishing another day. In the meantime you can play out here on the terrace where Brigitte can keep an eye on you.'

'Can't I even take Nikki for a walk?'

'No, play with him here,' Fabienne repeated. 'Then Brigitte won't have to worry about you. Is that understood, Michel?'

'Yes, *Maman,*' he agreed reluctantly.

'Or I could take him fishing,' Elise offered.

'Would you?' Michel put in excitedly, adding with a touch of doubt, 'But what about your new dress?'

'I don't expect it will take me very long to choose one. Then afterwards we'll walk down to the gardens by the river and you can fish for minnows.'

'I'll go and fetch my net and a jamjar,' he said eagerly, half slithering off his chair before remembering to ask, 'Please, *Maman*, may I get down from the table now?'

'Run along, scamp,' said Fabienne, affectionate amusement in her voice. As he disappeared inside the house, she asked Elise, 'Are you sure you don't mind? It is your time off, after all.'

'I'd like to spend the afternoon by the river,' Elise answered.

She was even quicker than she had expected in deciding on a dress. One in the window appealed to her, and she fell in love with it the moment she tried it on. In hyacinth-blue silk organza, it had a strapless bodice that dipped into a full dancing skirt, giving it an irresistible glamour.

The closely fitted bodice showed off the graceful line of her creamy shoulders and, standing in front of the full-length mirror in the changing-room, Elise couldn't resist holding out the skirt with her hand to let it fall with a silken whisper. It wasn't true what Luc had once said, that she was a clinical iceberg. Yet in her heart was the knowledge that even a month ago she wouldn't have chosen a dress that was so bewitchingly romantic.

The afternoon went quickly. In the shallow water near the sandy bank the minnows darted like golden fragments of light. Elise sat on the sunwarmed grass, watching Michel. A short distance away Nikki, who had bounded into the water, trotted back out with a stick in his mouth and shook himself vigorously.

'Look!' Michel exclaimed as he ran up to Elise to show her his jamjar again. 'I've caught another one!'

'How many is that now?' she asked as she studied the jamjar.

'Eight,' he said proudly.

'Eight?' she repeated so that she sounded impressed. 'That makes a very good afternoon's fishing.'

'Does that mean it's time to go?' Michel asked.

'I'm afraid it does,' she laughed, getting to her feet and shaking out her skirt. 'Shall we tip the minnows back now?'

'Do I have to? Can't I take them home and show Brigitte?'

'The minnows would be much happier in the river.'

Michel thought for a minute. Then he agreed, 'All right. I can tell Brigitte how many I caught, anyway.'

Crouching down where the river lapped the bank, he carefully emptied the contents of the jamjar back into the water. His tousled dark hair glistened in the sunlight as, absorbed, he watched the minnows dart swiftly away.

It flashed into Elise's mind that some day when Chantal was Luc's wife she would have a little boy like that, a son with alert eyes that mirrored his interest in everything around him. The pang that went with the wayward thought surprised her and, not wanting to dwell on it, she hurriedly took herself in hand.

Calling to Nikki, she fastened his lead. Then, with Michel chattering away happily, they walked back through the well-laid-out gardens, joining Fabienne just as she was about to close up the boutique.

On the way home the little boy wanted to tell his mother all about their afternoon. He had obviously enjoyed himself thoroughly, and Elise smiled at his enthusiastic account.

There was little traffic on the roads, and the countryside was tranquil in the golden light. The white buildings of the stalwart farmsteads stood out amid the patchwork of wheat, maize and vines. The draught through the open sun-roof ruffled her hair. Poppies grew thickly among the ripening wheat.

Had it not been for Richard she would have felt carefree and relaxed. She frowned a little, brushing a wisp of hair away from her face. Richard surely had to be responsible for most of her emotional turmoil, but she was conscious, too, that her row with Luc hadn't helped.

Bernard had left the Mercedes parked on the gravel drive, and as Fabienne drew to a halt behind it she remarked, 'The English buyer must be here. I expect he and Luc are already discussing business, but I think I'll interrupt to say hello as I'm going out this evening.'

Lately Claude had become almost as frequent a visitor at the château as Chantal, and Elise guessed Fabienne was having dinner with him. She knew that Fabienne valued his friendship, and from the way his gaze always lingered on her it was obvious that he cared for her a great deal. She was pleased that things were going well for them, but her heart sank at the thought of dinner. It was going to call for far more self-possession for her to survive the evening as one of only three round the dinner-table, and she wished that Fabienne, instead of going out, had invited Claude as an additional guest.

But at least it sounded as if Richard had arrived alone. She knew she should be thankful that she hadn't got to steel herself to meet his wife. Yet even so she found the prospect of joining the two men in the drawing-room before dinner daunting enough.

Richard had hurt her badly, and it was to stiffen her courage that she took trouble to look her best, not because she intended that he should see what he had thrown away. As usual her appearance was understated, but her pleated aquamarine dress enhanced both her slimness and the beauty of her colouring. She brushed her fiery hair to shining smoothness and pinned it up sleekly. Fastening the clasp of her turquoise pendant, she decided she was as ready for this ordeal as she was ever going to be.

Although she looked attractive and poised, she hesitated outside the drawing-room doors. Her heart was thudding nervously and she would have liked to have fled back upstairs. Instead her chin lifted determinedly and she walked into the room.

Richard got politely to his feet, astonishment coming into his face as he recognised her. Luc remained seated, his crutches by his chair. Elise was dimly aware of him, dark and urbane, his blue gaze impassive. His hawk-like surveillance, which she sensed rather than saw, somehow contrived to put her still more on the defensive.

It was the advantage of being prepared that helped her manage a composed smile. Her voice even, she began, 'Hello, Richard.'

'Elise—I can't believe it!' he exclaimed with a marvelling laugh. There was neither shame nor embarrassment in his voice, merely surprise. 'What are you doing here?'

'Working as a physio.'

'How are you?'

'I'm fine,' she answered lightly.

'Your parents are keeping well, I hope?'

When she thought of everything Richard had once meant to her, she could hardly believe she was carrying on this impersonal, slightly stilted conversation with him. But she not only answered him, she even heard herself enquire pleasantly, 'And how's your wife?'

Her question was met by an instant's taut silence. Then, with a slight twist to his mouth, Richard said, bitterness behind the casual tone, 'I'm not married.'

Her lips parted in surprise. Struggling to take in what he had told her, she was scarcely aware of him saying to Luc, 'I must apologise, Monsieur de Rozanieux. I should be speaking French, but Elise happens to be an old friend of mine.'

'So I believe.' There was an edge of dryness in Luc's voice. He went on, 'But please, don't apologise. I'm quite happy for us to talk English this evening.'

Elise's eyes sparked with resentment as she stared at him. She had no idea that her patient was fluent in English, that he'd understood every word she and Richard had just exchanged. Was there no keeping any part of her life hidden from him? she wondered with a stab of annoyance.

Defiance against him made her determined he wouldn't see how confused she felt. Six years ago Richard had told her he had fallen in love with his boss's daughter. He had broken off their engagement so that he and Suzanne could get married. So why had the wedding never taken place?

But even more puzzling than that unanswered question was her reaction to seeing him again. She had expected the desolation in her heart to be almost more than she could stand, and instead she felt oddly detached. Was it shock, or had she been so dreading this evening that it was bound to be an anticlimax?

But with the conversation over dinner to keep track of there wasn't time to probe her feelings. Her gaze strayed again to Richard as he addressed a remark to Luc. He still looked just the same, and she had no idea why she should find herself comparing the two men.

Both were tall and dark, but Richard's eyes were grey, and there were no midnight-blue highlights in his well-cut hair. There was still something faintly boyish about him, and that alone put an end to any similarity between him and her employer. Virile masculinity was stamped into every line of Luc's physique, and even at his most urbane there was a quality of fierceness about him that Richard had never possessed.

And yet she was wrong in thinking that Richard hadn't changed. She noticed the frown lines between his brows, the hint of disillusionment around his mouth that was new. Once she had admired his confidence; now she found his manner bordered on the brash. The observation drew her up with a jolt. What was she doing, thinking this way? She still loved her ex-fiancé, didn't she?

'I've never visited this part of France before,' Richard remarked as he helped himself to sugar and stirred his coffee. 'I always thought, though, that I'd enjoy touring the area.'

'There are certainly a lot of places locally that are worth a visit,' Luc answered. 'If you'd like to fit some sightseeing in during your stay here, I'm sure I can find someone to act as your guide.'

'Actually,' Richard said with an easy smile, 'I was hoping that Elise might have time to show me around.'

With a lift of a dark brow, Luc directed the question to her to answer. Had she not known him so well, she wouldn't have caught the faint glint of derision in his blue eyes, but, as so often, it was all it took to spark her hostility.

She knew exactly what he was thinking—that if she had any pride she'd tell Richard she was too busy to spare the time. For some reason their silent clash of wills prompted her to do exactly the opposite. She said, 'I was thinking of driving to Blois tomorrow afternoon. We could go together if you're free then.'

'Fine,' Richard agreed.

She used the excuse that she was sure the two men would want to talk business to leave them as soon as she'd drunk her coffee. To behave with her usual poise had taxed her to the limit, and she desperately needed to be alone to sort out her thoughts.

She went into the drawing-room and then wandered out on to the terrace. Moths flitted in the dusk. In the silence, the petals of a full-blown rose fell without a sound to cascade on to the stone balustrade. Elise picked one of the petals up, feeling its silky texture between her fingers, and suddenly, with total clearness, she knew that she no longer loved Richard.

It didn't seem possible that the magic was no longer there, but he was unmarried just as she was, and her heart should have been full of crazy hopes about there being a chance for them to find happiness again. Instead she had sat through dinner without her pulse so much as fluttering when his grey eyes had smiled at her.

The discovery pushed her dangerously close to the brink of another that was far more shattering. Luc was disturbingly attractive, and the whole time she worked with him she had to guard against his masculine charisma. But it didn't mean that to have fallen out of love with one man she must have fallen in love with another.

That would be madness. Not only was Luc engaged, but she was half expecting that the announcement would be made on Saturday at the party, which made it just as well that she had learned on no account to fall in love with a patient.

Yet she wasn't so convinced that she didn't spend a

sleepless night, and there was a tenseness about her the next morning as she gave Luc his session of treatment. Three short months ago she had felt completely in charge of her life. Now her emotions seemed perpetually in chaos, and twice she had to ask Luc to repeat what he had said to her. It didn't improve his temper.

'Will you stop acting as if you're in a trance?' he snarled.

'I'm not in a trance,' she protested.

'You've been in a romantic daze ever since you discovered that your ex-fiancé is still single,' he said scathingly. 'I suppose you're dreaming about the two of you getting back together again.'

Only too glad to smoke-screen her feelings from him, Elise answered, 'So what if I were?'

His dark brows came together with impatience.

'How can you be so naïve? Have you forgotten that Richard Kempson jilted you?'

'No, I haven't forgotten,' she said. 'And I haven't forgotten either how much he once meant to me.'

'So you'll give him another chance,' he said disgustedly.

'Why shouldn't I if I want to?'

She was trying her hardest not to be fiery, and it wasn't working. She had never been in a relationship with a patient that was as highly charged as the one they shared. Not only did she not know how to deal with it, but she didn't want Luc probing her feelings. She was too afraid of facing up to them herself.

His derisive blue gaze pinned her.

'I'm beginning to think some people ask for the blows they get dealt in life,' he said. 'Why don't you take a long, hard look at the facts? The truth is that Richard never loved you. Open your eyes, Elise. He wasn't the right man for you then, and he isn't the right man for you now.'

She stared back at him icily. She had no intention of continuing with this conversation. Keeping her tone even with difficulty, she said, 'Call me when you're ready to continue with your exercises.'

'Come back here.'

He didn't have to raise his voice to put a command in it.

Elise turned, her green eyes dark and turbulent.

'If I'm so wrong, why do you object to listening?' he demanded.

'Because you're a cynic!'

'Or perhaps I've more experience of the world than you have.' He sounded curt, and he paused as though trying to moderate his tone with her before he went on, 'Kempson is a guest in my house, and because of that I don't want to speak against him, but neither do I want to see him hurt you.'

'Why? Do you intend having the sole prerogative?'

'That's a stupid remark to make when I'm trying to talk to you!' he exploded.

'You *don't* talk to me—all you do is issue orders.'

Her accusation was unjust, but she wasn't in a mood to care. Luc's grip tightened on his elbow crutches. There was more than a suggestion of angry impatience in the set of his jaw, yet his voice was no more than forceful as he said, 'I'm well aware that I've done my share of shouting at you and giving you orders. But in between the arguments we've had, we've come to know each other very well. It's thanks to you I'm walking again, so it's hardly surprising that I care what happens to you.'

'I don't want your impersonal concern!' she flashed back, too angry to deduce why at this moment she felt so furious with him. 'In any case, I can look after myself.'

'If you could look after yourself, you wouldn't have been taken in by Kempson's brand of self-assured charm in the first place,' Luc told her. 'Good lord, has it never occurred to you that for him to know he wanted to marry Suzanne he must have been cheating you throughout your engagement?'

'Yes, of course it's occurred to me,' she snapped. 'I'm not *that* naïve!'

'Then if you're determined to make a fool of yourself twice, I won't try and stop you,' he said shortly, closing the subject.

Thankful when their session finally came to an end, Elise had to take a long walk through the grounds of the château before she even began to calm down. She could run her life quite adequately. She didn't want or need paternal advice from Luc, however well-intentioned.

And yet deep down she knew she had behaved unreasonably with him. Their friendship was such that it was only natural that he wanted to prevent her from being hurt. Not so very long ago she had been touched by the kindness he had shown her over her broken engagement. Now that same kindness made her all ready to lash out at him. Nothing had seemed right between them since that day a week ago when they had argued at the pool and then she had slapped him during therapy.

The phone in the study was ringing as she went back into the house. She was about to go upstairs when there was the sound of it being knocked to the floor. The ringing noise stopped abruptly, followed by a louder and much heavier crash.

Elise's heart skipped a beat and she sped across the hall, flinging the study door open to see Luc sprawled in an ungainly heap beside his desk. The phone, the receiver off its cradle, lay within an arm's reach of him. From the angry scowl he gave her he wasn't hurt, merely cross with himself.

She flew to him as he grabbed hold of the side

of his desk to lever himself into a sitting position. Admiration and annoyance at his stubbornness produced a curious ache in her heart. Dropping to her knees beside him, she exclaimed, her voice husky, 'Do you have any idea of the scare you've just given me? What were you trying to do?'

'What do you think?' he growled, impatiently flicking away the flex that had fallen across his legs. 'I was trying to answer the phone.'

'But your crutches are over by the bookcase.' She frowned. Comprehension came suddenly into her eyes, and she went on, 'Now I see. The phone rang and you thought you'd walk over to answer it without them.'

Her reproof was met by unrepentant sarcasm.

'You should have been a detective!'

She sat back on her heels, a light that was almost exasperated tenderness in her eyes.

'Are you hurt?' she asked.

'My pride's a little dented,' Luc answered gruffly.

Compressing his lips together, he made a second attempt to haul himself to his feet.

'Fold your arms across your chest and I'll help you,' Elise told him.

He did as she requested and, going to stand behind him, she went down in a full crouch. Sliding her hands through his arms so that she had firm hold of him, she took a deep breath and succeeded in yanking him upright. It took every ounce of her strength, and she was glad when he grabbed hold of the edge of the desk to relieve her of his weight.

The muscles in his arms bunched and she put a hand against his chest to help him steady his balance.

'Can you stand without me?' she asked breathlessly.

His brows came together as he looked down at her. The blue fire in his eyes almost mesmerised her, and he lifted his hand as though to gently graze her cheek. But the next instant a wintry chill was back in his face. Grabbing hold of her by the wrist, he thrust her away from him.

'Pass me my crutches and stop asking stupid questions,' he said curtly.

His rough dismissal of her stung, especially when a moment ago they had seemed on the point of repairing the rift between them. Going to the bookcase, Elise said, her tone sharp, 'I only hope that this has taught you that you've got to take things in stages. How would you have managed if I hadn't been on hand when you fell?'

She should have known that her question was tactless. Luc, more than any man she had ever met, hated being dependent on anyone. Unable to move because he needed the desk for support, he said scathingly, 'Believe it or not, I'd have staggered to my feet without your ministerings. I'm not paralysed any more, in case you've forgotten.'

'But you're not fully recovered either,' she retorted, handing him his crutches. 'Why can't you accept that, instead of pushing yourself all the time? In another couple of months you'll be walking without either crutches or a stick, if you haven't broken a leg first with your stubbornness!'

'Not everyone is blessed with your endless patience.'

As she was about to retaliate to his sarcasm, the quiet voice behind her made her start.

'There's a phone call for you, Monsieur Luc,' announced Brigitte.

Focused so strongly upon each other, neither of them had heard her come in. The interruption in their exchange made Elise realise how close they had been to a physio-patient clash developing into another fiery personal argument.

With a sense of frustration and despair, she turned and walked from the room.

CHAPTER EIGHT

RICHARD was standing leaning against the Renault, his jacket thrown casually over his shoulder, when Elise came down the steps from the house.

'I didn't realise I was keeping you waiting,' she began.

His eyes travelled over her. She was wearing a patterned beige and white skirt, teamed with a summery short-sleeved cotton top and white slingback shoes.

'I'm not complaining.' He smiled, opening the car door for her. 'In any case, the way you look, you're worth waiting for.'

She gave him a cool glance as she slid behind the wheel. Already she was more than half wishing she hadn't agreed that he could accompany her. She would have felt much freer exploring Blois on her own, and she had no wish to have him flirt with her.

Her tone was a shade businesslike as he got in beside her.

'I thought I'd like first of all to go round the château at Blois,' she said.

'That's OK with me,' he answered. 'Frankly, as long as we have the chance to talk, I don't mind how we spend the afternoon. I know I treated you badly six years ago, but I'd like us, if we could, to be friends.'

'We can try,' she agreed.

'Good,' he smiled, settling back in his seat as she started the car.

Elise was relieved to find that the conversation between them during the drive was easier than she had expected. Richard asked her about her work, and she talked to him in some detail about Stoke Mandeville, the hospital she'd moved to shortly after they had split up. She gathered that his career had progressed well too, though apparently it hadn't been as meteoric as he would have liked.

The tour of the château lasted just over an hour, and they were strolling across the vast sunlit quadrangle towards the exit when Richard remarked with a slight frown, 'You know, you've changed. You're far more cool and collected than you used to be.'

'You only think so because I'm not crazily in love with you any more.'

'You sound very sure of that,' he said with a question in his voice.

'Do you really think I'm not sure, after the way you jilted me?' she asked.

His steps slowed to a halt.

'If it hadn't been for Suzanne——' he answered, before breaking off bitterly.

Elise glanced up at him, seeing in the bright sunlight the cynical lines around his mouth, and asked curiously, 'Why didn't you marry her?'

'Because she always had some reason for not setting a date for the wedding.'

'You mean you got tired of waiting?'

'No, what I mean is that about a year after we'd got engaged she told me it was all over. She'd met someone in the film world who was going to help her start an acting career.' His voice was harsh as he said, 'Stupidly, I thought I could win her back. I kept thinking it till I had a postcard from her telling me she was married.'

There was a pause, and then Elise said, unable to help the fact that she sounded stilted, 'I'm sorry.'

'So was I,' he said sourly as they began to walk

towards the exit again. 'I'd not only lost Suzanne, but in one fell swoop I'd also lost my chance of a seat on the board and of taking over eventually as the chairman of her father's company. It's not a setback you recover from overnight.'

Elise could hardly credit what he had said. So Luc, without ever having met Richard, had been right. Suzanne's attraction for him had been that she was the boss's daughter. Elise had been barely twenty-one when she had agreed to marry him, but even so she was staggered that she could have been such a poor judge of his character.

The evidence of his callous ambition must have been there even then, if only she had seen it, though certainly it had grown in the time they had been apart. His whole conversation, she realised, had consisted of money and his upward moves in the property market.

Perhaps if he'd never met Suzanne and had married her he wouldn't have developed into such a hard self-seeker. Elise was only thankful that she had been romantic enough to want to be a virgin for him on their wedding night. At least she hadn't had to get over the trauma of having slept with him.

It had been the strangest two days, and she was grateful for what she had learned from them, so it made no sense at all that she felt as troubled as before. Yet deep down she knew now what the reason was. It was the row she'd had with Luc a week ago. Not that she'd been the one who had caused it, she thought obstinately. But, when she couldn't get to sleep again that night, her sense of being the injured party was very little comfort.

She got up and, pulling on her wrap, paced restlessly over to the window. Luc had been angry when she'd helped him to his feet that morning and his gaze had been cold throughout dinner. Even if she made an attempt to heal the rift between them, he would probably reject it.

With a faint sigh she drew aside the curtains so she could see the tranquil, moonlit grounds. As she did so she noticed the parallelogram of light on the terrace that shone out from the study window. It was after midnight, and she was surprised that Luc was working so late.

She hesitated a moment and then, impulsively, made up her mind. If she waited until the morning she might not have the same resolve.

She went downstairs. The door to his study was ajar and she could hear the rustle of papers. For a second her determination faltered. Then, without knocking for permission to enter, she pushed the door open and crossed the threshold.

Luc, who was sitting at his desk, glanced up. The dark brows that lifted with surprise at the sight of her did not soften the patrician sternness of his features.

'What are you doing down here so late?' he asked, his tone curt and challenging.

Elise advanced a little way into the room, going to stand behind one of the Queen Anne style armchairs. Nervously she ran her fingers along the back of it.

'I couldn't sleep,' she faltered.

'That makes two of us,' he mocked sarcastically. 'What do you expect *me* to do about it?'

He was obviously not in a receptive frame of mind to listen to her, but in spite of it she persevered. 'I was hoping we could talk for a few minutes.'

'Try me some other time,' he answered, his voice preoccupied and dry. His gaze didn't lift from the papers in front of him. 'I'm too busy at the moment to play the part of the platonic friend while you discuss the traumas of your love-life with me.'

'That's exactly the response I'd have expected from you!' she flared, more emotion in her voice than she would have wished.

Luc glanced up.

'All right,' he growled, 'what is it? Now that you've interrupted me, you may as well get it off your chest.'

'I can't talk to you when you're in this sort of mood,' she retaliated, and felt her eyes begin to smart. Antagonistic sarcasm masked her hurt as she went on, 'I'm sorry if I've disturbed you while you're working, especially as it's not important!'

His sharp gaze narrowed on her. Reaching for his crutches, he got to his feet.

'I'm beginning to think it is,' he contradicted curtly as he came round his desk. 'You're upset about something.'

'No, I'm not,' she argued.

'Stop being so hostile,' he ordered. 'Now, tell me what's wrong.'

'Can't you guess?' she asked with a desperate kind of anger. 'It's us! We've been at daggers drawn ever since that day I slapped you.'

Luc breathed in deeply. He sighed, a latent fierceness in his steel-blue eyes despite the softening of his attitude.

'Both our tempers got out of hand that day,' he answered quietly. 'So let's forget it, shall we?'

'How can I,' she demanded, a lump in her throat, 'when things aren't the same between us any more? We had a good relationship until a week ago. Now there's a barrier between us. Even when I want to help you, like when you fell this morning, you're sarcastic and aloof. I know I shouldn't have slapped you, but you shouldn't have grabbed hold of me either . . .'

To her dismay she heard the rhythm of her voice falter and cease. Without waiting for her to go on, Luc rested one crutch against the side of his desk and stretched out his hand to her.

'Come here,' he said quietly, his voice roughened with tenderness.

Elise didn't question the telepathy of communication they seemed to share at that moment. Instead she crossed the room to go blindly into his embrace. Her fingers went to his hard neck, the ache in her heart dispelled by a wave of gladness so intense that she felt a tear trace down her face.

Luc held her close, the slight roughness of his jaw grazing the softness of her cheek. The faint scent of his aftershave was musky and evocative, conspiring with the iron feel of him and the possessive way he held her to heighten the bitter-sweet poignancy of the moment.

'I'm sorry I was so fiery with you that day,' she whispered.

'Don't be silly,' he murmured.

His warm hand ran up the curve of her back, coming finally to rest on her shoulder. Releasing her a little, he tilted her chin up. There was a hot glow in her tear-misted eyes, and as he looked down at her face his expression changed, as did the nature of their embrace.

She heard his hiss of sharply indrawn breath. As though he was unable to help himself, his fingers combed almost savagely into her hair. Her heart seemed to skip a beat as his intense blue gaze slipped to her slightly parted lips.

'You'd better get to bed,' he ordered, his voice harsh, yet husky. 'You're incredibly lovely, and that robe looks as if it would come off very easily. I haven't made love to a woman since the accident, so don't tempt me.'

A shiver seemed to run up her spine at his words, and her anger was all the fiercer because of it. Disregarding the dangerous force-field of tension that pulsed between them, and the way her heart was hammering wildly, she flashed back, 'Are you really so arrogant you think I'd let you seduce me?'

'Why don't we put it to the test?' he rasped.

Using the desk at his back for support, he snatched her against him. The contact with his hard male body momentarily took her breath away. By the time she had recovered her wits enough to struggle, it was too late. In a panic she pushed against his rock-like shoulders, making no impression at all as his mouth claimed hers in a kiss that held no savagery, but which was far from gentle.

A soft sound of protest and bewilderment murmured in her throat as a shudder of weakness and longing went through her. It was as though something long concealed within her ignited, to flame into answering passion. Her hands, which had gone to repulse him, sought the column of his neck and then tangled in his hair as she felt his lips part hers.

Her heart began to pound its thunderous beat throughout every inch of her. Pleasure ran like liquid fire along her veins as Luc's mouth explored hers and, before she even realised it, she was feverishly kissing him back. Her slim body was on fire, need for him a hunger in her blood that made her forget Chantal's very existence.

It was only when Luc's hand slid down her spine, pressing her even closer, letting her feel his arousal, that, shocked, she broke the kiss. Turning her head away, she gasped, 'Stop, that's enough!'

His lips found the sensitive hollow at the base of her throat.

'Oh, you're intoxicating,' he muttered.

'No,' she pleaded raggedly, desperately fighting to clear her pleasure-drugged senses so that her mind could tell her why this was wrong. 'No . . . please.

Luc, stop!'

His head lifted and in that moment, suddenly, Elise remembered that he was engaged to Chantal. Contempt for herself that she had let him kiss her with such intimate thoroughness brought a rush of colour into her face. With her eyes blazing, she twisted out of his arms.

'Don't touch me!' she exclaimed in a voice that trembled with fury.

Needing to reach out for a crutch to steady his balance, Luc couldn't grab hold of her wrist to pull her back close to him. His breathing was harsh and irregular, and his face set hard. Yet with almost a contemptuous indifference he taunted, 'What happened? Did you suddenly remember the inimitable Richard?'

Elise was so angry, she could feel herself shaking. Clenching her hands against their trembling, she hissed, 'You're despicable! How *dare* you ask me . . .?'

'You know, you do the outraged act very well,' he interrupted mockingly, 'especially when only a moment ago you were so willing and feverish in my arms.'

She looked at his maddeningly controlled features, the cold derision she saw in his blue eyes changing her anger into a tight knot of resentment. There was more than a touch of the aloof and imperious in his stance. Pain twisted her heart as she realised she would never have the same power over his emotions as he had over hers.

Glaring at him, she said with stony coldness, 'Think of it as all part of the therapy!'

For an instant Luc's mouth went tight. Then it quirked with cynical amusement. He didn't say anything—he didn't have to. She knew as clearly as if he'd said the words that if the passion that had flared between them had been therapeutic for anyone, it had been for *her*.

Certain that she would hit him if she stayed with him a second longer, she turned quickly. She felt the stab of his gaze between her shoulder-blades as his satirical gaze followed her out of the room.

The hem of her wrap billowed out as, crossing the hall, she broke into a run. Her heart was racing so hard, she had to pause at the head of the stairs to try to steady it. Yet, even now that she was safe from him, the night was still full of agitation and unrest.

Tentatively she brushed the tips of her fingers against her lips, which still throbbed with the sensuous pressure of Luc's kiss. A tremor quivered through her as, even while her mind rebelled against her feelings, her body remembered his nearness.

Clutching her wrap protectively to her, she made her way to her room, the anger in her at war with another emotion, one much stronger and far more frightening. She sagged against her bedroom door as she shut it, leaning her head back against the wood. Sometimes she thought she hated Luc de Rozanieux more than any man on earth. And sometimes, she finally admitted, closing her eyes against the sharp rise of anguish . . .

'So I'm not the only one who goes sneaking about after midnight!'

The sneering male voice, so unexpected in the stillness, made her gasp. Her eyes flew open to see Richard standing between her bed and the window, his hands in the pockets of his dressing-gown.

Still in a state of shock, she demanded, almost blankly, 'What are you doing here?'

'I came to see if you were still awake,' he said harshly. 'It was obvious at Blois today that there was something preventing us from understanding each other. I wanted to try to find out what it was. But now I see it's quite obvious. You've just come back from Luc de Rozanieux's room, haven't you?'

'I was with him in the study,' she answered.

'Were you really, now?' he jeered, before exclaiming, 'My, how you've changed! You were never generous with your favours with me. Now I find you granting them, unstintingly by the look of you, to your crippled patient!'

'Don't you dare use that word!' she flashed. 'Even when he was in a wheelchair, Luc was more of a man than you'll ever be. And for your information, he's engaged to the daughter of the local newspaper magnate whose party you've been invited to on Saturday. So you can keep your nasty assumptions to yourself!'

Richard stared at her for a minute. Then he muttered, 'I'm sorry—I take back the accusation. I should have realised that you have to check on his medication. It's just that, seeing you again I realise I still love you. It was infatuation with Suzanne. I must have been mad to let you go.'

'I don't think you ever loved me,' Elise told him in a clear voice, not the least bit moved.

'How can you say that?' he protested, taking hold of her by the shoulders.

'Quite easily,' she answered, breaking free from his grip. 'If you loved me, why did you never bother to get in touch with me after Suzanne left you?'

'I didn't know where to find you,' he said, throwing out his hands. 'You'd left the hospital where you used to work——'

'You had my parents' address!' she interrupted on a note of scorn.

'All right,' he conceded irritably, 'I *could* have contacted you. But the rest of what I've said is true.' He put his thumb under her chin and tilted her face up. 'You're a very desirable woman, Elise—perhaps even more desirable than you were six years ago. That defiant look you get in your eyes at times would be a dare to any man's virility. I find I still want you.'

She pushed his hand away.

'But I don't want you!' she retorted. 'And I certainly don't want you here in my room, so just get out!'

She went and opened the door wide, her eyes angry as she stood beside it, resolution in every slim line of her. Richard's expression hardened. Then he taunted, 'If it's your reputation you're worried about, then you'd do better not to come back from your patient looking as if you've been ravished. Not everyone knows, as I do, how Victorian your attitudes are!'

Elise tensed instinctively as he came nearer. But he made no further move to touch her as he went out. She closed the door behind him and, aware suddenly of how very frayed she felt, sank down on the bed.

Richard avoided her as much as possible over the next couple of days, though he was superficially pleasant when they met at mealtimes. Elise knew that nothing ever escaped the hawk-like perceptiveness of her patient and employer, but Luc made no comment or enquiry about her relationship with her ex-fiancé.

Neither did he refer to the flare-up of desire between them. Yet, as a result of what had happened, she found she couldn't be spontaneous with him. Not that she wanted to be. The greater the distance between them, the easier it was to refute the notion that she had fallen in love with him.

But, for all her refusal to accept the truth, Elise found it hard to master the jealousy she felt when Chantal joined them at the conclusion of their session in the pool. Giving Luc a jaunty little wave from the terrace, his fiancée ran lightly down the steps while he swam strongly to the rail.

'I thought with the party tonight you'd be too busy to come over this morning,' he began teasingly as Chantal bent down with supple grace by the pool's edge.

She was wearing a leggy dress in a vibrant collection of colours. Her sunglasses were pushed up on her head, where they rested smoothly on her shining dark hair, and Elise was ashamed of herself for thinking that it was a pity she didn't overbalance and fall in.

'My mother's got everything so well organised, there's nothing for me to do,' Chantal answered with a caressing little laugh. 'Am I interrupting your treatment, or can I stay and watch?'

'We're finished now, aren't we?' Luc said to Elise.

Keeping her voice even and brisk, she confirmed, 'Yes, that's all for this morning.'

He hauled himself out of the water while Chantal held his crutches for him. Elise watched and then swam in an easy breast-stroke to the steps, fighting the envy in her heart because it was Chantal who helped him, and not herself.

She climbed out of the pool as Chantal handed him a towel and asked, 'How's the therapy coming along?'

'Fine, as you can see,' he answered, adding, his voice amused, 'When are you going to stop worrying about me, my sweet?'

'Perhaps when I stop caring about you,' Chantal teased back. She pouted prettily. 'Besides, I can't help it. I was so terribly afraid you might never walk again.'

'I know,' he said.

There was a tender note in his voice that made Elise glad the session was over, or she would have found it hard to stop herself from picking an argument with him over nothing. Yet she knew it was herself she should be angry with, not him.

She must have been mad to lose her head even for a second that night, knowing that he was engaged to Chantal. To an experienced man like Luc, a kiss meant nothing. He no more loved her than Richard had done, and the sooner she bludgeoned her turbulent feelings for him back into control, the better.

She didn't realise how intently she was watching him with his fiancée until she saw him glance at her. Something flickered in his eyes as he met her turbulent gaze. Then, bending his head, he deliberately brushed Chantal's lips with his.

'I won't be long changing, and then I'll join you out here for coffee.'

'Fine,' purred Chantal.

With the muscles rippling in his shoulders, Luc went towards the house. His gritty determination meant that he was now adept with the elbow crutches, and they in no way detracted from his dark good looks or the impression he gave of strength and vitality. Elise could never remember feeling quite so unreasonably angry with anyone as she watched him depart after kissing Chantal. Unless she could get her emotions back in check, she realised she was going to have to tell Dr Dercourt that, for personal reasons, she couldn't continue any longer with the case.

Chantal sat down on one of the wrought-iron chairs and crossed her long, tanned legs. Elise hesitated. It went bitterly against the grain to have to ask Chantal for her help to stop Luc from overdoing things. But she had put off mentioning the problem to his fiancée at least twice in the last few days. Now, determined to prove to herself that despite everything she could still be detached and professional about her patient, she began, 'Can I talk to you for a minute?'

'Of course,' Chantal said haughtily, twirling her

sunglasses between her fingers. 'What is it?'

'It's about Luc,' said Elise, and congratulated herself on how very in control she sounded. Not one flicker of how difficult jealousy was making this for her was evident from her tone. 'The improvement he's made these last few weeks has been amazing. But he's still not as mobile as he'd like to be, and patience isn't one of his strong points. A couple of days ago he fell, and in my opinion he's pushing himself too hard.'

'You mean he could put back his progress?' Chantal said sharply, frowning as she demanded, 'Well, why haven't you spoken to him about it?'

'I've tried repeatedly to get him to ease up,' Elise told her, 'and I'd try again if I thought it would do any good. But if *you* asked him, it would obviously carry more weight.'

'I'll talk to him as soon as he joins me, but I *wish* you'd told me about this before.'

'As yet, no harm's been done.'

'That's what——' Chantal began, before breaking off and saying with an irritable shrug, 'It doesn't matter. I'll talk to him, though if you were any good at your job, he'd listen to your advice.'

Managing somehow not to rise to the provocation, Elise left her and went indoors.

The party that evening was to start at eight. She showered and then, sitting at her dressing-table in her lace briefs and strapless bra, she painted her nails with silver-pearl varnish. Since she was going to wear evening sandals she did her toes to match. Her sheer, blue-mist stockings toned beautifully with her dress and, as she walked over to the mirror, she felt the gossamer caress of the fabric as it swirled about her.

Looking at her reflection, she asked herself yet again how she could have been so stupid as not to have realised much earlier that she was getting far too involved with Luc. She still wouldn't admit it was love. If she did, her heart would begin to ache unbearably.

Why hadn't she heeded Dr Dercourt's warning and taken stock of her emotions weeks ago? Then she wouldn't be feeling like this, hurt and raw and angry with Luc because all she was to him was a competent physio.

It gave her a pang to wear the earrings he had given her, but out of a sort of defiance she slipped them on. Pride made her determined that there would be no crack in her composure when his engagement to Chantal was announced tonight. No one was going to guess her thoughts, and perhaps, if she went on acting as though she was calm and unruffled, she might even will herself back to sanity where her patient was concerned.

Picking up her silk fringed shawl and evening bag, she went downstairs. Fabienne and Claude had already left together for the party, and Richard was on his own in the drawing-room. Fate seemed to have conspired to make him Elise's partner for the evening. Luc, assuming that they were going to the party together in the Renault, had said he would see them there.

'I'm not ready yet,' Richard announced tersely. 'I've got to put a phone call through to my boss. Monsieur de Rozanieux drives a hard bargain, and before I commit myself I want to check that it's OK.'

'I'll wait for you by the car,' Elise said.

'I just hope this doesn't take too long,' he replied. 'Saturday evening isn't the best time to get hold of my boss. I don't know why Monsieur de Rozanieux couldn't have put his cards on the table earlier.'

'He has a reputation for being a tough man to beat in business.'

'Yes, well, so do I,' snapped Richard, obviously fed up that he hadn't got a more favourable deal.

Leaving him to make the call, Elise went outside. The last of the sun's rays were touching the château. The breeze was warm, and she strolled a short distance along the drive so that she could admire the view of the sunset.

When she heard a man's tread on the gravel she turned round, expecting it to be Richard. Instead it was Luc, dark and devastatingly urbane in a white shirt and dinner-jacket. She had never seen him in evening clothes before, and she felt her heart jolt at his attractiveness.

Instead of getting into the Mercedes, he came towards her. The austere blackness of his suit made her very conscious of the compelling edge of fierceness that was stamped in his character. He had all the sexual magnetism of virility, power and success, and her chin lifted as she struggled to keep from succumbing to her feelings for him.

His masculine gaze appraised her as he halted, leaning on his crutches, and for an instant there was a strange flaring of the static in the air. Then he began, his jaw set and his tone clipped, 'I want an explanation from you now that we've a few minutes alone. What did you mean by upsetting Chantal this morning?'

It was always with *her* that he was so critical. Never once had he used that clipped tone with Chantal. But, adept at concealing her emotions, Elise sounded imperturbable and cool as she answered, 'I didn't upset Chantal, and I don't know how you got the impression that I did. All I said to her was——'

'What you said to her was enough to have her in tears with me,' he cut in ominously.

She meant to defend herself calmly. Instead she suddenly flashed with an anger that took her by surprise, 'Perhaps she enjoys getting your sympathy!'

Luc's blue gaze narrowed on her face. 'Do I detect a slight note of jealousy?' he drawled mockingly.

The taunt was too much for her. She erupted, 'What a typically conceited remark!'

'And from you, what a rare display of temper,' he returned. 'If I were conceited, I'd almost think I'd hit a nerve.'

Her eyes were stormy, and her breathing quickened with the sheer effort of denying him the satisfaction of a heated response. He gave her time to answer and then, when she didn't avail herself of it, ordered brusquely, 'I hope it is now understood, you are not to interfere between me and Chantal again.'

'Perfectly,' she snapped.

CHAPTER NINE

THE CHARRONS' house was virtually a mansion, Elise thought, as, having been welcomed by the newspaper magnate and his wife, she and Richard went out into the gardens. Music drifted through the open french windows of the ballroom. Groups of guests were gathering on the terrace and lawns, while formally uniformed waiters with trays loaded with champagne glasses circulated unobtrusively. Already the buzz of conversation and laughter promised a most scintillating night.

'Old Monsieur Charron must be worth a packet,' commented Richard, respect and envy mingled in his voice. 'You know, if your patient were to marry Monsieur Charron's daughter, the two families would be just about able to buy up the whole neighbourhood between them!'

Elise took a sip of champagne and didn't answer him. Her eyes were dark, and she felt as brittle as the glass in her hand with the effort of pretending to herself that she hadn't fallen hopelessly in love with Luc. She was certain that his engagement to Chantal was going to be announced tonight, and, from the stab of pain she felt on hearing Richard's remark, she wondered how she was going to stand the anguish of it all.

'As you've been at the château several months,' Richard went on, 'you must know quite a few of the people here.'

'I do,' she agreed as she smiled a hello to one of the town councillors and his wife. 'Now that Luc's on his feet again, he entertains fairly frequently.'

152

'Then you can tell me who the influential people are and perhaps introduce me to some of them. It's always useful in this world to make the right kind of contacts.'

'Do you ever think of anything other than getting ahead?' Her remark was automatic and shaded faintly with contempt.

'Of course I do,' he retorted.

At that moment Luc appeared on the terrace. Despite the clusters of guests on the long lawn that separated Elise from him, the babel of conversation and Richard's voice close beside her, some sixth sense seemed to alert her immediately to his presence. She glanced up, seeing that Chantal, looking stunning in a flame-coloured dress with a black bodice, was at his side.

The dress was cut low and was very fitted, showing off her shapely figure. A cunning slit in the skirt revealed a glimpse of thigh, and after years in the modelling world Chantal knew exactly how to move to heighten the impression she gave of indolent sexiness.

Elise, with her burnished auburn hair and expressive, long-lashed eyes, had her own form of haunting beauty. Yet, studying Chantal and Luc, she knew exactly how Jane Eyre had felt witnessing Mr Rochester with Blanche Ingram.

From where she stood she could see the impact they had as a couple on the people around them. Heads turned and attention shifted. The compulsion of Luc's personality meant that people inevitably gravitated towards him. Elise knew it would have been the same even had he been confined to a wheelchair for life, such was his magnetism.

She realised that Richard had spoken to her and she hadn't heard him. She forced her attention back to him.

'I'm sorry—what did you say?' she asked.

'I said I spend a lot of my time thinking about us,' he replied shortly. 'Unfortunately, you don't seem to be interested.'

A waiter walked by and Richard helped himself to another drink. She didn't want to have to spend the whole evening with him just because they'd arrived together, and as he turned back to her, she said, 'Let's mingle.'

It turned out to be easier to lose him than she had anticipated. She was standing with a group of people, talking to a local wine-grower and his wife, when one of Chantal's brothers joined them.

Elise had met Philippe socially a couple of times before. In his late twenties, he was tall, indolent and amusing company. Taking her hand, he tucked it through his arm and led her away from the group before she could protest.

'I've decided to rescue you,' he announced with his humorous smile.

'What from?' she laughed.

'From my father's friends. They're charming people, but much too staid for someone like you. Come and be part of the younger, noisier set until we go in for dinner.'

No one watching them as they strolled across the lawn together would have believed that Elise wasn't completely happy and relaxed. And she was determined that no one should guess. But only part of the act that she was putting on stemmed from pride. Another part stemmed from the knowledge that, if she didn't make a supreme effort to keep the ache around her heart suppressed, the pain would become intolerable.

As she went up the steps to the terrace, she passed near to the laughing group that Luc and Chantal were with. She glanced sideways and her eyes inadvertently met his, and she was momentarily taken aback by the fierce sparks in them. Despite having reprimanded her earlier, he was obviously still angry with her. Chantal must have completely twisted what she had said.

Lanterns came on in the gardens as the twilight deepened, and people began to drift into the ballroom to take their seats for dinner. Elise had been placed on the same table as Richard, though several seats away from him.

'I'll see you later,' Philippe said with a smile as he left her to join his family and their close friends at the main table.

Her dinner companions were interesting and easy to talk to. Yet in spite of her resolve Elise couldn't help her gaze straying periodically to Luc and Chantal. With a familiar ache beneath her ribs, she noted that he made the perfect foil for Chantal, his dry wit and undertone of firmness pairing well with her staginess and sparkle.

Coffee was finally served, and the photographers from the local paper edged closer to the main table in readiness for the moment when Monsieur Charron stood up to address his guests. The chandeliers were dimmed, the band stopped its gentle background music, and an expectant hush quietened the hubbub of noise and festivity.

His speech was pithy and entertaining. In it he referred to his wife, his family and to the newspaper he had run for forty years. Some spontaneous banter between him and some of the newspaper staff who were seated on a nearby table caused yet more laughter.

The toast was proposed and drunk, then Monsieur Charron held his hand up again for silence. In his resonant voice he declared, 'And now it gives me great pleasure on such a happy evening to announce a piece of news which I'm sure some of you have been expecting.'

Elise felt her grip tighten on the slender stem of her glass. She sat completely still, so tense beneath the façade of calm that she scarcely seemed to breathe as she waited for the blow. Monsieur Charron continued, 'Two people we all know and love have announced tonight that they plan to get married.'

He paused for dramatic effect, and Elise, her throat tight, glanced at Luc and saw him smile. Her heart flinched as a muscle would from the surgeon's knife.

'So I want you all to join me in a toast to . . . Fabienne and Claude!'

She gave a little start of astonishment and her glass almost slipped from her numbed fingers. Amid the applause she scarcely heard her companion's approving comment, but mechanically she made the right reply. As the band played a snatch of the Wedding March from *Lohengrin*, she rallied and joined in the clapping.

Fabienne and Claude were still being showered with congratulations as Monsieur and Madame Charron stood up to start the dancing. Skirting the dance-floor that was quickly filled with other couples, Elise went up to the main table to give her good wishes to the newly engaged pair. She kissed Fabienne who, in a slim white column of a dress, looked radiant, and then turned to Claude, who embraced her continental fashion.

'The two of you are made for each other,' she declared warmly. 'I'm so happy for you both.'

'Thank you,' smiled Fabienne, her eyes alight.

Philippe's hand touched Elise's back lightly.

'Just the woman I was looking for,' he said. 'Can I persuade you to dance?'

'Without any trouble at all,' she laughed.

Claude and Fabienne's happiness was infectious

and, like a prisoner unexpectedly granted a release, suddenly she wanted to dance and have fun. The music was right and, with the crystal chandeliers dimmed, the floor was full of movement and romantic shadows. Elise went out on to the floor, then turned to face Philippe, giving him a brilliant smile.

She was still a little dazed that somehow the inevitable hadn't happened, and her carefree mood showed in the way she danced. Fluid yet vibrant, she was worth watching. Her skirt wrapped tightly around her ankles and then uncurled like a blue flower as Philippe twirled her towards him and then spun her away. He was as good a dancer as she was, and together they made an eye-catching couple.

Yet she didn't notice that she had the close attention of two dark men, one on the main table and one at her own. She felt light enough to want to dance all night, and Philippe clearly had no intention of parting with her. Luc's engagement to Chantal was still not official, and . . . And what? she asked herself.

The question brought her back to reality. At the same moment the tempo slowed and Philippe drew her close. She put her arms around his neck, her thoughts far away and her eyes troubled. Whatever the reason for delaying the announcement of their engagement, Luc and Chantal obviously shared a close understanding.

Tonight had altered nothing. Over the next weeks, until Luc was completely recovered, Elise would go on treating him. They would continue to clash and make up while she fought an endless war with her feelings. Only how much longer could she expect to carry on before those feelings tore her apart?

'Do you mind if I cut in on you?'

Richard's voice was curt as he tapped Philippe on

the shoulder. Without waiting for an answer he
elbowed him out of the way, and Elise found herself
being pulled abruptly into his arms. Several of the
couples nearest to them glanced in their direction.

'Richard, you're making me conspicuous!' she
snapped in a furious undertone.

'Well, perhaps I'm a little tired of having you
neglect me,' he taunted. 'We came together, if you
remember.'

His close-pressing hands meant that her body was
pulled into a tight fit against his. He was making
them look like lovers, deliberately staking a claim to
her. Repelled by the intimacy that was being forced
on her, she whispered fiercely, 'Richard, stop it!'

'What's the matter?' he enquired softly, refusing to
release her. 'You never used to object when we
danced like this.'

'I'm objecting now!' she said angrily, pushing
against his shoulder as he bent his head to kiss her
temple.

His mouth curved mockingly at her reaction.

'I'm not so sure any longer that I was wrong with
my first guess about you and your patient,' he jeered.
'Tell me, is it him you're saving yourself for?'

She felt angry colour flame in her face as she
retorted, 'Luc is a gentleman. Not only is he always
in charge of himself, but he would never push me
into making a scene.'

Heeding the veiled warning, Richard stiffened and
released her. Turning away from him, Elise walked
off the dance-floor to go back to her seat.

She was stopped when a hand shot out and caught
hold of her wrist. She looked up into Luc's glittering
blue eyes. In a quiet voice that spoke volumes, he
demanded, 'What was that all about?'

Her chin went up. Her face was still flushed, her
poise shaken, and the pressure of the evening had

been such that she felt in no shape to tangle with him over Richard or anything else. Feigning calm, she said, 'What was what all about?'

He laughed softly. Then, with a steel-like firmness to his words that she was only too familiar with, he said, 'No, Elise, you don't try that one on me.'

Though neither of them had raised their voice, the electricity between them was so forceful that already they were attracting speculative glances.

'Let go of my wrist,' she insisted. 'People are looking!'

'Then let's go somewhere where we won't have an audience.'

She knew from his tone that he wouldn't stand for any opposition from her. Much as she resented being coerced, she allowed him to escort her out on to the terrace. They walked a little way. The music still drifted to them on the breeze, but they were alone.

Turning to face him, she said, her voice even but a spark of rebellion in her eyes, 'I'd like to get back to the party, so what is it you wanted to say to me?'

'You've been having a good time this evening, haven't you?' he said, a slight sneer in his voice.

'Do you object to that?' she asked coldly.

He made her tremble inside. At one time she would have thought it was with anger. Now she knew better, and it made her all the more defensive.

'No, I don't object,' Luc said in a harsh tone. 'But your ex-fiancé obviously objects most strongly to watching you play hard to get.'

'I haven't been playing hard to get!' she protested. 'If you're referring to the fact that I've spent a lot of the evening with Philippe, I happen to like his company. And in any case,' she went on, becoming angry, 'what business is it of yours how I choose to behave?'

'You're my employee,' he ground back, 'and that

makes it my business.'

And that was all she would ever be to him: a competent physio who had helped him to walk again and who in his better moods he felt a warm sense of gratitude to. The stinging reminder of the nature of their relationship was a stab of anguish that made her retaliate.

'And it was *my* business this morning when I spoke to Chantal about the way you've been pushing yourself with your therapy. You told me not to interfere, so I'll tell you the same thing now! My relationship with Richard is *my* affair.'

She went to walk past him, but he caught hold of her, bringing her close to his chest. His crutches were hardly an encumbrance to him any longer, and unless she wanted a bruised wrist Elise couldn't snatch herself free.

'You should have told me you were planning to make Richard jealous tonight,' he mocked.

'What do you mean?'

'I mean I'd have done a better job for you than Chantal's brother.'

She pushed at his shoulders as swiftly he bent his head. Her protest was muffled by his mouth as it claimed hers with an almost cruel fierceness. For an instant the world seemed to tilt dizzily. She knew he was punishing her and she tried to fight him, yet the truth was that she welcomed even this harsh caress.

The rigidity of her slim body softened and, as it did so, Luc switched the kiss to a sensual demand. With a hopeless sense of despair Elise knew she was responding to him. Her heart was pounding with excitement, the hot fire of longing racing through her veins. Luc's hands slid up between her shoulder-blades, pressing her breasts to the hard warmth of his chest. She made a soft sound of bewildered pleasure, her fingers tangling in the crisp hair at the nape of his neck.

In the flame Luc had kindled everything was melting: the antagonism she had so often marshalled as her best defence against him, her cool decisions to keep a tight rein on her emotions, the illusions she had cherished right up to this evening that she could, despite her love, treat him with medical detachment. Even when she had been engaged to Richard she had never felt like this about a man, but then she'd never known a man like Luc.

A louder snatch of music drifted to them, and suddenly out of the spinning madness some measure of sanity came back to her. The insanity of what she was allowing made her panic.

'No!' she gasped against his mouth.

With the last of her strength she pushed at his shoulders. Pulling free from his arms, she stared at him with dark, shocked eyes, and without the stone balustrade at her back she didn't think her legs would have supported her.

In a choked voice, she demanded with all the vehemence of deep pain, 'Why are you so hell-bent on hurting me? All I ever wanted was to help you, to see you walk again, and you're paying me back by making it impossible for me . . .'

A sob snatched the end of the sentence away. Luc took hold of her arm. He was breathing hard, his face intense, but she never knew what he intended saying, for footsteps sounded on the terrace.

'Please . . .' she whispered desperately, imploring him to release her so that she could regain control of herself before they were interrupted.

His strong fingers tightened and then released her. She turned to face the balustrade, thankful for the shadows that hid the shine of tears in her eyes. To the person approaching she knew it would look as though she and Luc were enjoying a quiet moment of solitude together.

'I've been looking for you, Elise,' Philippe began easily. 'I didn't realise you were out there. Do you mind if I steal her away for a dance, Luc?'

'Not at all,' answered Luc, adding, the gibe in his voice too subtle for ears other than her own, 'It's a pity to waste the music.'

But, although she went back into the ballroom with Philippe, Elise danced with him to only two more numbers. He tried to persuade her she must stay longer and then gave in with good grace, telling her that he had enjoyed the evening with her.

Richard was sitting alone at their table when she returned to it to collect her evening bag, fingering his glass. He got to his feet.

'Since we came together,' he said levelly, 'I assume we're leaving together.'

'As long as it's understood that I'm doing the driving,' she returned.

'Are you telling me I'm drunk?' he snorted.

His tone was certainly a shade more biting than usual, but he was accustomed to drinking heavily, and the champagne and after-dinner brandies seemed to have had little effect on him. But since Elise was completely sober she wasn't taking any risks.

'All I'm saying,' she answered, 'is that I'd be happier at the wheel.'

Despite what had happened on the dance-floor, it didn't occur to her to feel nervous about being alone with him as they walked to where the Renault was parked beyond the swimming pool and tennis courts. She had once been engaged to him, and she thought she knew him.

He was sullen during the drive along the country roads, rebuffing Elise's attempt at conversation. She gave up, and the sound of the car engine seemed to intensify the silence. Overhead in a dark sky, unscreened by clouds, a bright moon was casting pewter-toned shadows over the resting vineyards and silvering the distant river.

She was glad when she turned off the road into the tree-lined avenue to the château. She was aware that Richard had been watching her steadily in the glow of the dashboard and, though she didn't show it, his brooding gaze was making her uneasy.

Suddenly he said sarcastically, 'Tell me, when did you first decide you were too good for me?'

'I don't know what you mean,' she answered.

'Oh, yes, you do,' he said with a harsh laugh. 'Now that you're mixing with the millionaire league, it's very clear how high your sights are set—on Luc de Rozanieux, no less.'

'Luc's my patient,' she told him. 'There's nothing else between us.'

'Is that a fact?' he mocked, adding gratingly, 'I saw the two of you disappear out on the terrace together tonight, and I've watched the looks that flash between you. What else do you give him apart from his treatment?'

'Stop being so unpleasant!' she said sharply.

Though the grounds of the château were floodlit, the house itself as it came into view was all in darkness. Elise realised suddenly how isolated she was with Richard, and a prickle ran over her skin, as though something brushed it lightly in warning.

'What was it you told me?' sneered Richard. 'That even in a wheelchair your patient was more of a man than I am?'

'You said you hoped we could be friends,' she said, her voice steady though her heart was beginning to thump with an awareness of danger. 'Please, let's not argue.'

She slowed to a halt on the gravel drive and

switched off the engine. Wanting to reach the safety of her room, she moved quickly to open the car door.

'Not so fast,' snapped Richard. 'I haven't had a goodnight kiss yet.'

'Let go of my arm,' she demanded. 'You're hurting me!'

'You've played hoity-toity with me once too often,' he grated. 'If a cripple's your idea of a good lover, perhaps I ought to show you what it can really be like!'

She wrenched her arm free, but before she could push the car door open he grabbed hold of her, flinging her back against the seat. Momentarily the breath seemed to be knocked out of her by his roughness, and the acid smell of wine on his breath made her turn her head away sharply as he leaned over her.

'You fastidious little bitch!' he muttered thickly as he jerked her chin towards him with cruel fingers. 'I should have taught you a lesson when you ordered me out of your room.'

'Don't touch me!' she hissed, then she closed her lips tightly as his mouth covered hers.

Fury, fear and disgust fused together, making her struggle all the more wildly. Revulsion was so fierce in her, she thought it would choke her. Richard's lips ground against her teeth, his weight pressing down on her and, unable to contain her panic, she fought him with all the strength she possessed. Wresting one of her hands free from his vicelike grip, she clawed out blindly at him.

Her nails caught him across the cheek. He swore savagely, manacling her wrist again before deliberately raising his other hand and slapping her. She gave a brief, muffled scream and he snarled, 'Go on acting the wildcat and you'll see what else you get for it!'

She heard the ripping noise as he fumbled with her bodice, and she tried to bite him, her frenzied writhing only exciting him further. Her breath was coming in panting sobs, and with a desperate effort she managed to press her hand against the horn before he struck her again.

Unable to escape his violating hands, she became distraught. She knew she was losing, her strength no match for his. His palm was clamped over her mouth as he tore her bodice to the waist. In her anguish and terror she was scarcely aware of the powerful car headlamps that suddenly illuminated the interior of the Renault.

But moments later the passenger door was yanked open and a man's hands grabbed hold of Richard, hauling him out of the car so that she was free. She pushed her own door open and stumbled out, her legs giving way beneath her so that she fell to her knees on the gravel.

She didn't see Luc's fist draw back and then pound into Richard's jaw, sending him sprawling on the ground. Crouched into a defensive ball, she began to cry in terrified sobs, scarcely aware of the footsteps that came running as Bernard raced over from where he had slewed the Mercedes to a halt, or of Luc's curt instructions to him.

Elise was in the grip of such wild fright that when a hand touched her shoulder she flinched, staggering to her feet and backing against the car.

'Elise, it's me—Luc. It's over now.'

She stared at him, her eyes dark in her pinched face, before she burst into tears of relief. Leaning on one crutch to steady his balance, he enfolded her in his arms, and with a muffled, tearing sob she buried her face in his shoulder, desperate for the protection and comfort of his lean, powerfully muscled body.

It was a long while before she steadied and stopped

trembling. Gently Luc held her away from him a little, his fingers tightening on her shoulder as he looked down at her. The intense blue of his eyes held something she was too shaken to understand, something deeper than pain and stronger than anger. She had never seen him look so grim or sound so quiet and capable of violence as he said, 'What happened? What did he do to you?'

'He . . . he grabbed hold of me . . . when I stopped the car,' she managed jerkily. 'I tried to get away, but . . . but he wouldn't let me go.' Fresh tears came into her eyes as, still desperately shaken, she moved back into his arms. As they tightened around her, she whispered, 'I was so frightened. If you hadn't come when you did . . .'

She shuddered, and she wasn't sure what he muttered in relief. His palm smoothed her hair that had come loose in the struggle and now fell about her shoulders. Gently he eased her away from him and reached into the driving seat for her silk shawl. He draped it around her and she blushed, painfully realising for the first time how badly her dress was torn.

'I'd better get you indoors,' he said. 'You look as if you might faint.'

'Where . . . where's Richard?' she asked huskily.

'Bernard is driving him to the station. He won't ever touch you again.'

There was something in his tone that made her shiver, and she clutched her shawl more tightly to her as though the warmth could stop her trembling.

Luc saw her to her room. He pushed her gently on to the bed while he went into the bathroom. She had never felt so frighteningly weak. Her throat seemed raw and her cheek burned painfully where Richard had slapped her.

Joining her, Luc took her tangled hair back from her

face, pressing a cool wet towel to her bruised jaw. Then he tended to her cut mouth, ministering to her as carefully and competently as any medic.

The gentleness in his strong hands meant that she wasn't prepared for what she saw in his gaze when she glanced up. His dark brows were drawn together thunderously and rage burned in his eyes.

Immediately she pushed his hand away, stood up and snatched the towel from him.

'You don't have to look after me!' she snapped in a voice that was far from steady. 'I don't want you looking after me, not when you think what happened was my fault.'

'What in heaven's name . . .?' he demanded, grabbing hold of his crutches and getting to his feet, his dark scowl confirming how right she was. Beneath the grim calm he was furious with her.

'You accused me of playing hard to get at the party,' she flashed. 'You think I led Richard on, don't you?'

'I do not think you led him on,' he corrected her between clenched teeth.

'Then why are you so angry with me?' she challenged.

'I'm not!'

'Yes, you are,' she cried. 'Do you think after all this time I can't tell when you're angry with me? You think I asked for what happened!'

'Heavens!' he exclaimed in frustration. 'What do I have to say to convince you? I don't hold you responsible in any way.'

'Then you're blaming me because I've jeopardised the business deal you and Richard had just worked out,' Elise persisted.

'Damn the business deal!' he exploded, snatching hold of her by the forearm and pulling her towards him. 'Do you think I care about anything except——?'

He broke off, curbing his temper, and going on in a voice that was fiercely controlled he conceded, 'You're right—I'm angry. I'm good and angry. I saw the way that bastard danced with you. I knew he'd been drinking heavily, and I should never have let you leave with him.'

Elise's eyes misted as she looked up at him with sudden comprehension. Impetuously she ran her hand along his jaw. Then in a husky whisper she demanded, 'How can you possibly blame yourself? You arrived in time, that's all that matters. And I'm not hurt.'

'Not hurt?' Luc repeated tersely. 'Your dress is so badly torn you'll never be able to wear it again, and your shoulders are covered in bruises. If anything worse had happened to you, I don't think I could have lived with it.'

'But it didn't,' she whispered.

'No, thank heavens,' he said, taking hold of her fingers and kissing the tips. 'If you're not too shaken, a bath would soothe your bruises.' She nodded and he went on, 'While you're taking it, I'll get you a drink to help you sleep.'

When she came out of the bathroom in her nightgown he was setting a cup down on her bedside table, and she wondered how he had managed to carry it when he needed both his crutches on the stairs.

'I believe the English resort to tea at the culmination of every crisis,' he commented, the note of amusement in his voice restoring the first glimmer of humour between them in some while.

Elise smiled, but her throat felt too tight for a reply. Luc sat down on the bed while, propped against the pillows, she took a sip of the scalding liquid before exclaiming with a little laugh, 'How much brandy did you put in this?'

'Enough to make you sleep,' Luc answered with his attractive smile.

She took another sip, aware of him watching her and somehow not daring to raise her eyes to his. It felt strange to have him caring for her like this, a curious reversal of roles that made her suddenly want to start crying again. Fighting the upsurge of emotion, she said huskily, 'Isn't it wonderful about Fabienne and Claude?'

'I think Claude's been in love with her for years,' Luc answered. 'And he'll make an excellent father for Michel.'

'Michel's very fond of him,' she agreed.

She finished the tea and Luc took the cup from her. As he did so, she noticed the rawness across his knuckles and breathed, 'What did you do to your hand?'

'I socked your ex-fiancé on the jaw,' he said, dismissing her concern. His mouth tightened. 'At that moment I could have killed the rat!'

Elise shivered with delayed reaction and Luc put an arm around her.

'Are you all right?' he enquired gently, dropping a kiss on her forehead.

'I think I drank the brandy too fast,' she confessed in a whisper.

He moved, and she had the impression that she was falling as he leaned back, drawing her down with him against the pillows so that she lay in the warm shelter of his arms. Her heartbeats seemed to echo strangely in her head, yet dizzy as she was her senses stirred with drowsy excitement at the close physical contact with him.

Without knowing what she was doing she slid her hand beneath his shirt as she turned her cheek against his chest. But the tremor of restraint in his arms and his quick intake of breath made no impression on her. Already she was deeply asleep.

CHAPTER TEN

JUST over a week later Elise was being shown into Dr Dercourt's consulting-room to inform him of a decision she wished she had taken when she had first realised how intensely involved she had become with her patient. Then she might have escaped the agony of wanting Luc's love and knowing that she would never have it.

But it was the nature of their relationship since the night of the party which had pushed her into finally taking the step. The morning after, at breakfast, Luc had asked her if she wanted the day off. But apart from that no mention had been made by either of them of Richard's attempted rape of her.

When she gave Luc his therapy, she was quieter than usual but still unshakably professional. In return he was scrupulously polite, despite the clenched set of his jaw. Yet the tension between them seemed constantly at snapping point.

Elise understood that Chantal had left for a modelling assignment in Monte Carlo and would be away for some time. Presumably that accounted for the simmering irritation and frustration she sensed in Luc. But instead of snarling at her and skinning her with his sarcasm, as he certainly would have done at one time, he treated her with the most infinite restraint.

She felt she would explode with rage and heartbreak if she had to endure any more of his impersonal consideration. It was all she could do not to yell at him that she wasn't Limoges porcelain. Quite obviously the situation could not go on. Dr

Dercourt offered her coffee, but, though they chatted inconsequentially until it was brought in, she could tell from the way his sharp, diagnostic eyes stayed on her that he knew she had come to discuss a problem with him. Wanting to get it over with, she announced as soon as his receptionist had left them, 'Claude, I want to be taken off the case. I'd like to return to England.'

'I hope nothing's wrong at home?' he asked immediately.

Elise managed a frayed smile.

'No, it's nothing like that,' she said. 'I just don't feel able to continue with the case any longer.'

'But why?' he asked with a puzzled frown. 'You've been so successful getting Luc to walk again. Surely you want the reward of all your hard work by staying until he makes a complete recovery?'

'Please,' she said tightly, 'don't ask me for my reasons.'

The doctor hunched his shoulders expressively as he insisted, 'I can't help but ask, if only out of concern for the well-being——'

'If I thought Luc's full recovery hinged in any way on me, then I'd stay,' she interrupted. 'But a replacement could take over from me quite easily at this stage.'

'Yes,' he conceded, 'a replacement *could* take over, but I know absolutely what Luc will think of the idea. Have you told him?'

'No,' she admitted, 'I haven't, not yet.'

Dr Dercourt stood up. Coming round from behind his desk, he drew up a chair beside her, talking to her as a friend.

'We've known each other for a long time,' he said. 'Now tell me, what's the problem?'

'Can't you guess?' she said with a wan smile.

'No, frankly I can't,' he answered. 'If you'd come

to me when Luc was still confined to a wheelchair and you were taking the brunt of his scathing comments, I could have understood it perfectly. It was because he was being such a ferocious tyrant, and there was a doubt that he'd walk again, that I wanted you as his therapist. He would have cowed anyone else. But that's history now and anyone can see the rapport the two of you have established. Which leaves me completely at a loss to know why you want to be taken off the case.'

'I can't go on treating Luc because——' She broke off and then confessed in a sudden rush, 'Because I've fallen in love with him. That's why I have to get away. I just can't cope with my feelings for him any more and carry on as his physio at the same time.'

'So that's it!' Dr Dercourt exclaimed quietly. 'Well, yes, you're right, I ought to have guessed. Luc has a lot of drive and a very magnetic personality, and the two of you have worked together very closely.'

'Just as I've worked closely with other attractive male patients in the past,' Elise said as she stood up and paced towards the window. She gave a short, impatient sigh. 'I ought to have been too professional to get so involved.'

There was a pause, and then Dr Dercourt enquired, 'Have you considered what Luc's feelings are for you? I'm sure you mean a very great deal to him.'

'I mean as much as a physio always means to a patient she's been successful with,' Elise answered. 'But it's Chantal he's engaged to.'

'Chantal? That's news to me.'

'It's unofficial, and will be, I imagine, until Luc has completely recovered.'

Her voice wasn't as steady as she would have liked, and Dr Dercourt came and put a sympathetic hand on her shoulder.

'My dear, what can I say, except that I'm sorry?'

'Can you arrange for my replacement to take over from me as soon as possible?' she asked, striving to be brisk about the matter.

'I'll see to it that you're free to leave this coming weekend.'

Her heart contracted at the thought of only three more days at the château. But with outward composure she said, 'Then I'll start making my travel arrangements straight away.'

'When are you going to tell Luc?' the doctor asked as he escorted her to the door. 'If it would help, I'll do it for you.'

'No, I'll tell him,' Elise said huskily.

Remembering that she had tried to give in her notice once before and Luc had torn up her letter of resignation, she delayed speaking to him about her decision until the very morning she was leaving. He had a business appointment at ten o'clock in Montpierre, and Bernard had already brought the Mercedes round to the front of the house when she knocked on the study door and went in.

Luc was collecting some papers from his desk and he turned as Elise came in, leaning on the stick he was using now instead of crutches. He was more stubborn and tenacious than any man she had ever known, and the sight of him, tall and powerfully shouldered in a charcoal grey suit, made her heart begin to ache. Her eyes took in the straight line of his jaw, the satirical black brows, the steel-blue eyes. He meant so much to her. Yet her pride demanded that he shouldn't see how much she loved him. She couldn't bear it if she broke down and cried. He would be pitying and kind, and the agony of desolation would be even worse.

'What are you hovering in the doorway for?' he demanded tersely when she didn't speak immediately.

'I'm not hovering,' she told him, forcing the words past the constriction in her throat. 'I wanted to speak to you about something. It . . . it's important.'

He glanced at his watch and said curtly, 'Then make it fast. I'm off in a couple of minutes.'

His remark made hot anger suddenly surge up inside her. She was about to say goodbye to him, to walk out of his life completely, and he was almost too busy to listen to what she had to say! Her eyes sparking, she flashed, 'I'm giving in my notice!'

She had his full attention now. Frowning at her, he demanded harshly, 'What's brought this on?'

Elise fought to bring her emotions back under control, succeeding in making her voice calm and even, so that it gave no indication of the strain she was under. 'I'm handing in my notice for personal reasons that I'm not prepared to discuss with you.'

The reasons were that she was tearing up inside with the pain of loving him, that she was so desperately unhappy she didn't know how she was going to bear being apart from him, but that to stay would be a torture even worse.

'You may not be prepared to discuss them now,' he said raspingly, 'but I'm telling you you're damn well going to talk about them, and in some detail, when I get back this afternoon.'

He walked to the door, and clenching her nails into her palms, Elise said quietly, 'I shan't be here when you get back.'

Luc paused to shoot her a threatening look from under lowered brows.

'You'd better be,' he said grimly, before continuing on his way out.

She heard the sound of his footsteps as he crossed the hall, and then a few minutes later the roar of the Mercedes' engine. Her chin began to tremble and she caught her lower lip between her teeth. She would not cry; she would not cry! Any form of goodbye would have been a knife-thrust of pain. But it was better to part with no display of sentiment, better to go out with sparks than with a whimper.

Determined to be controlled to the last, she packed with hospital-like efficiency, refusing to give in to the turbulent impulse to hurl everything into her suitcase and then in tears to cram it shut. The cramping ache around her heart waned to a dull misery as the taxi which had called for her picked up the main road to Tours, leaving the familiar landmarks of the de Rozanieux estate behind.

The train wasn't in when she arrived on the station platform. She bought a couple of magazines, sat down on a seat and forced herself to read. It didn't matter what the articles were about so long as they stopped her thinking about Luc.

From the very moment she'd met him he'd turned her life upside-down, destroying the cool, collected image she had been so proud of, wrecking her calm, stirring up in her indignation and anger because of the ease with which he guessed her thoughts. She hadn't even been able to hide her broken engagement from the sharp probe of his mind.

But now she was going back to England, to a life she had worked hard to build and which would surely eventually deaden the ache of desolation. After a few days at home with her parents she would move back into her flat, look through the physio journal for a stimulating and challenging new post, perhaps even branch out into a field other than spinal injuries. For an instant the charm seemed almost to work. Then despair cast it aside. How could she have twice made the mistake of falling in love with a patient?

Trying to calm her thoughts, she pictured the countryside that she loved so much around Oxford.

In her mind she could see her parents' mellow honey-coloured house gleaming a welcome in the sunshine. But the image failed to comfort her. Instead she felt worse, until the wretchedness of being separated from Luc seemed practically to engulf her.

It was the clanging of the train as it pulled into the station, and the bustle of the people around her, that made her realise how completely her concentration had wandered from the magazine that lay open on her lap. Picking up her luggage, she walked a short way alongside the train and then climbed aboard.

There was plenty of room and the compartment she chose was empty. She sat down in a corner seat, facing the engine, impatient now to put an end to the prolonged pain of leaving. Her fingers drummed on the armrest. She glanced at her watch. More doors slammed further down the train. Some passengers banged along the narrow corridor with their luggage on their way to the next compartment. But still the train didn't move.

Elise looked at her watch again. It must be slow, or else the train would have pulled out by now, but the station clock would show the right time. Pushing open the sliding door of the compartment, she went out into the corridor and walked to the exit.

She was so intent on trying to make out the position of the clock's hands at the very far end of the platform that it was with a start of shock that she felt herself being grabbed hold of and jolted forward. Losing her balance, she half fell, half stepped off the train to look up in astonishment at Luc.

'What are you doing here?' she gasped.

'I could ask you the same question,' he fired back, his voice holding an incisiveness that bordered very close on sarcasm.

There was an implacably stern look on his strong-featured face and a hawklike fierceness in his blue eyes. He was angry, and yet somehow, with an immense effort, keeping the force of that anger in check. Elise felt her heart begin to beat unevenly and turned her head away, knowing she must control her expression.

'I'm going back to England,' she managed in a slightly muffled tone.

A nerve jumped in his clenched jaw as he retorted, 'If I'd had any idea you were serious this morning when you said you were quitting, I would not have gone into Montpierre. Luckily Brigitte had the sense to phone and tell me you'd left with your luggage, or I'd have come home to find you gone with not one word of explanation. As it is, you and I are going to talk things through.'

Elise was conscious of a slight jolt of panic and began to feel angry. She had done her level best to say goodbye to him with quiet dignity and calm, and here he was undermining all her stoical intentions, insisting on an explanation she was equally determined not to give.

'There isn't time to talk things through,' she said, her chin lifting defiantly. 'My train's due out at any minute.'

'Yes, but you're not going on it,' Luc snapped grimly. Keeping hold of her arm, he moved her away from the train door. 'I'll get your luggage off for you and then we'll go somewhere so we can talk.'

Her voice rising, she declared, 'I'm not going anywhere with you! You try to take my luggage off the train and I'll call a porter! Dr Dercourt has arranged for another physio to take over. I've done what I was engaged to do. I've fulfilled my obligation, and that means that now I'm free to go.'

'That's where you're wrong,' he said savagely, taking hold of her by the shoulders and only just managing to stop himself from shaking her. 'Now, for heaven's sake, stop stalling and tell me what this is all about!'

From somewhere further up the platform a door shut with a final sound and the train made a jarring noise.

'I've told you as much as I'm going to,' stormed Elise, 'and you've bullied me for the last time. My mind's made up—I'm leaving! Now, let go of me or I'll miss the train.'

'So you're going back to that bastard who tried to rape you!' Luc exploded with fury. 'What's wrong with you that you can't get Richard out of your system? Are you hellbent on destruction?'

She was aware of the open door to her carriage edging past and, glancing up, she saw that the train was already moving. Struggling to pull away from Luc, in desperation she shouted back, 'Even if I were going back to him, it would be better than eating my heart out over you!'

Luc's brows came together. One second his eyes were sharp with angry incomprehension, the next they were ablaze with a hot, leaping light and, in a frenzy of dismay, she realised what she had said.

'Let go of my arm!' she demanded frantically.

'Not till you tell me what I think I just heard,' he insisted huskily.

Knowing that she was crying, in pure desperation Elise snatched herself free. Luc made a grab for her but was too late, and she began to run along the moving train towards her carriage door.

'Come back here, you little fool!' Luc shouted after her furiously. 'Haven't you realised yet . . . ? I love you!'

She reached up to catch hold of the side of the door and jumped aboard. Tears were streaming down her face and, trembling, she turned to see that Luc had broken into a limping run.

'Elise, listen to me . . .' he demanded.

'I won't come between you and Chantal,' she called back in a choked voice as, for an instant, he came almost abreast with her below her on the platform.

Then the train, ever gathering speed, widened the distance between them. He gave up trying to keep pace with her. Slowing to a halt, he shouted with angry tenderness, his words only just reaching her above the noise of the wheels, 'You fool! I'm not engaged to Chantal!'

Elise stared at him in bewilderment. The wind was whipping past her and the track starting to go by so dizzily and fast, it was no longer safe to stay in the open doorway. She took one more look at where he stood, arrogant and alone on the receding platform, and then wrenched the door shut.

Her legs felt so weak that with the jolting of the train she hardly knew how she made it back to her compartment where she collapsed into her seat. She closed her eyes, still able to see Luc with her inner vision as he had stood on the platform, the emotion in his face almost paralysing her.

He had called after her that he loved her. He had shouted three magical words she had thought without any doubt she would never hear from him. Elation began to surge up inside her. She was going to get off at the next station. She was going back to him. If he was no longer engaged to Chantal . . .

And then reason began to still the wild upsurge of hope and happiness. She didn't know what had put an end to his engagement with Chantal, but she did know all about the bond that developed between patient and physio, the bond that came from fighting against difficult and sometimes impossible-seeming odds, and winning.

Opening her eyes, she turned her head to the window, watching as the houses that crowded close to the line sped by and then gave way to open countryside. She and Luc had experienced so much together, wasn't it natural he should think he was in love with her, in the same way that Richard once had?

Suppose she went back to him, and suppose, she thought, feeling cold, that in time he discovered that all he had really felt for her had been a dangerous combination of affection and fiery sexual attraction? She would sooner end things now, however painful, than face the agony of breaking up later on.

She was right to be returning to England, right to be distancing herself from a relationship that was too intense for either of them to see it as it really was. Yet the rhythm of the wheels on the track, incessant, denying every solid-seeming argument she put forward to justify what she was doing, kept beating out, 'You're running away, you're running away, you're running away.'

Her father was at Heathrow to meet her. They drove home along the motorway in the evening sunlight. At any other time Elise would have enjoyed the drive, chatting easily to her father. Now her thoughts were troubled and unhappy. If she was so utterly certain she had made the right decision, why did she feel so wretched, confused and lost?

'You're very quiet, love,' her father commented. 'Are you tired after the journey?'

She was more than tired. She felt exhausted. Perhaps after a night's sleep she would see things more in perspective. And perhaps, came the interrupting thought, she'd treated her emotions like symptoms to be dealt with and not listened to for much too long! Perhaps it was time she finally faced up to the challenge of being a woman!

But it wasn't at that moment that the realisation of what she had to do dawned. It was later, after dinner. She had gone upstairs and was unpacking when her mother joined her. Sitting on the end of the bed so that they could talk, she began, 'One of the things that's guaranteed if you work as a nurse is that you either fall in love with one of the doctors or one of the patients.'

Elise turned from the wardrobe, the dress she had been about to hang on the rail still in her hands.

'Oh, heavens!' she exclaimed huskily. 'Is it that obvious that I'm in love with Luc? I thought I was putting on such a brave front!'

Despite her expression, that was full of anxious concern, her mother smiled.

'You were,' she agreed, 'but normally over dinner you'd have discussed the medical side of the case, at least in the most general terms.' She paused, and then went on quietly, 'I wish it could have worked out for you this time, *ma petite.*'

'It's my own fault that it hasn't,' Elise answered, her voice throaty. She came and sat down on the bed, groping for the words, because it was only as she spoke that things were at last becoming clear to her. 'You see . . . I think Luc loves me. Only when he told me this morning at the station I wouldn't listen. After the way Richard hurt me, I've been so afraid of being vulnerable again . . . too afraid to take even the slightest risk. And then it was all so sudden, what Luc said . . . and the train was pulling out. I couldn't believe it, or take it in. So . . . I ran away.'

She finished in a cramped whisper. Her mother gave her arm a reassuring squeeze.

'From what you've just told me I don't think you need to be upset. Your letters made Luc sound a very determined and dynamic man, and men like that go after what they want. When he knows where you are, he'll come and find you.'

In a voice that held the sudden ring of decision, Elise answered, 'He won't have to. Because tomorrow I'm going back to him.'

She smiled out at the billowing clouds as the plane winged its way from Heathrow airport to Paris. The torment and indecision were over. She was going to tell Luc how she felt.

As the plane began its descent she imagined his surprised reaction when she called him from the airport. He would never think she was phoning him from Paris.

But it turned out that she was the one who was surprised. Having cleared Customs she came out into the vast arrivals hall. Passengers swirled and eddied about her, and it took her a moment to get her bearings and to start to walk towards the line of phone booths. And then, suddenly, she stopped in amazement.

There, tall and authoritative, so that he stood out from the press of people around him, was Luc. He saw her at the same moment as she saw him, their eyes meeting across the crowd, his expression telling her everything she needed to know. She paused for an instant, knowing that the step she was about to take was the most momentous of her life.

Then, abandoning her luggage, she ran forward, lithe and laughing, her green eyes alight, her whole face vivid with the glow of the joy she felt. Luc met her half-way, crushing her in his arms, holding her so tightly that she could scarcely breathe.

She felt so choked with happiness, all she could manage was a whispered, 'I love you.'

It was more than enough. Holding her away a little, he looked down at her as though wanting to imprint every feature indelibly on his mind. Then, with the flame of passion and devotion in his eyes, he bent his head, kissing her with a hunger as though he was appeasing an eternity without her.

Oblivious of the crowd that surged about them, Elise kissed him back, rapture quivering through her at the feel of his mouth on hers and the live, warm strength of the arms that held her as if never to let her go.

When finally Luc released her a little and raised his head, they were both smiling, and she knew that they had finally found the perfect understanding that had been there all along, just out of reach.

'Let's get your luggage,' he said, his voice a shade rough with emotion. 'As soon as we get out of here, there's a question I want to ask you.'

'There's one I want to ask you too,' she said with a breath of laughter, her arms still linked around his neck. 'How did you know to meet me?'

'My question is the more important of the two,' he said, his eyes intent on her face. 'Are you going to marry me?'

'You make it sound like an order,' she said, tenderly amused.

His eyes laughed. Brushing her lips with his with such loving gentleness that she felt herself go weak, he murmured huskily, 'It is an order. I can't live without you. That's why as soon as I got your number I phoned your home to say I was coming to England. But your father told me you were already on a flight to Paris.'

CHAPTER ELEVEN

THE LIGHTS from the bridge up ahead were reflected in the Seine, sending shivers of brightness rippling over the water. In the distance the Ile de la Cité, crowned by Notre-Dame, stood out against the night sky, bathed in an ethereal golden glow. From the bank came the soft lapping sound of water against stone. The noise of the traffic seemed safely remote, scarcely impinging on the charm of the river.

Elise slipped her arm through Luc's as they strolled along by it with the unhurried pace of lovers.

'Happy?' he asked softly.

She glanced up at him and smiled back.

'Incredibly happy. I can hardly believe that only yesterday I thought you were going to marry Chantal. It's been such a whirlwind of an afternoon. You still haven't told me what happened between you and her.'

Luc looked down at her, tender humour in his blue eyes as he said, 'I was never engaged to Chantal.'

'But . . .' she faltered uncomprehendingly.

'I'd no idea till the day you drove me to the winery that Chantal had made out to you that the two of us were engaged.'

'Then if it wasn't true, why didn't you tell me?' she said with a protesting little laugh.

He grazed her temple with his lips, sounding both amused and rueful as he answered, 'It suited me to let you think it. I hoped I just might get some flicker of jealousy out of you.'

'You certainly did!' she commented with feeling. 'I had to try the whole time to hide it.'

'And there was I thinking you had no interest in me apart from as a professional physio,' he said, so that she laughed.

'But there was *something* between you and Chantal,' she persisted after a moment. 'You were always so understanding with her.'

'I felt I had to be. She's very highly strung and dramatic. Before the accident we'd had the sort of on-off relationship that thrived when we were together and died when we were apart. There was no depth to it; we both knew that. But after I'd pulled her out of the crash and was paralysed, she seemed to think she had to devote the rest of her life to me, whether I wanted it or not. I knew how guilty she felt because she'd escaped unhurt and I hadn't. I was worried, and so was her father, that it was going to push her into having a complete breakdown. The kindest thing I could do was to avoid any great drama, and to prise her gently away from me.'

'So that's why you were angry when I talked to her about your progress,' said Elise, suddenly understanding.

'Yes,' he smiled, his arm going round her. Keeping her in the shelter of his embrace, he went on, 'I'd finally convinced Chantal that she should accept the modelling assignment in Monte Carlo, which will be good for her career. Then the morning of the party she sobbed in hysterical tears that she wasn't going. It took me a long time to calm her down and finally to make her see that I didn't need her at the château, that even if I'd remained confined to a wheelchair following the crash she still wasn't under any kind of obligation to me.' He paused and then added, a teasing note to his voice, 'Does that answer all your questions about me and Chantal?'

'All but one,' Elise said softly. 'Since you were never engaged, when did you first realise you were in love with me?'

'It wasn't a realisation,' he told her. 'It was a *coup de foudre*. I knew I wanted you from the first moment I laid eyes on you. You were kneeling down at my feet, adjusting the wheelchair, your hair alive with copper glints in the sunshine, and then you looked up at me with those cool green eyes. What I felt was as sudden as a flash of lightning. It was an instantaneous discovery that you were the woman who'd been created for me, the one I'd always been waiting for, my Eve.'

His words held her spellbound, they were so precious. She halted and turned to him, the street-lamp nearby casting its radiance on her upturned face. Marvelling, she said in a husky voice, 'And I'd no idea. I thought . . . I was so sure . . .'

'I can guess what you thought, the way I raged at you,' Luc said drily, pausing before going on, 'I was in a wheelchair and, because that made me doubt my manhood, I was insanely jealous the whole time. I wanted to possess you, every thought, every emotion, so much so that I even accused you of making a set for Claude, even though in my more rational moments I knew absolutely it wasn't so. It was torture having you near me, having you touch me with your caressing hands and yet knowing you were unobtainable. You infuriated me with your special brand of self-sufficiency and your calm coolness, and what made it even worse was that I knew there was such fire underneath, a fire you were perhaps saving for some other man. You were on my mind every moment. Even when I slept I couldn't stop dreaming about you.' He sighed, his thumb slowly stroking her cheek. 'You woke me from one of those nightmares.'

'But I thought your nightmare was about the crash.'

'The nightmare was about you, you standing in the drive with a tractor coming towards you that you hadn't seen. With my useless legs I couldn't push you clear to save you. I couldn't move.'

'Oh, darling!' she whispered, awed and yet aware that her love for him was no less intense than his for her.

'You obsessed me,' he murmured, taking her hand that had gone to caress the line of his jaw and pressing a kiss to its palm. 'And the frustration made me into an arrogant tyrant, which in turn made me all the more wild, because I knew I was making it impossible for you to even like me.'

'You're so wrong,' she said huskily. 'It was you as the arrogant tyrant that I fell in love with. I'd seen courage before, but you were so indomitable and determined. I admired and loved you so much. Besides,' she added, her eyes full of tenderness, 'have you forgotten how caring and protective you were with me at times? The night of the party——'

'Oh, don't rub salt in that wound!' Luc interrupted with a ragged laugh.

'What do you mean?'

'I mean that I still feel responsible. You see, it was because of me that you and Richard came face to face again.'

'You mean . . . you engineered it?'

'Not in any Machiavellian way,' he answered. 'It came about quite easily. For some time I'd been interested in getting another English importer to take some of our wine. When the company I was negotiating with arranged to send a representative to the château to thrash out the details, I had the strong suspicion it was your ex-fiancé. A few tactful enquiries confirmed it. The only thing that surprised me was that he wasn't married. I was terrified of losing you, but at the same time I hoped that if

Richard came to the château and you saw him again, you might discover that you'd idealised your relationship with him.'

'You were right,' she told him. 'As soon as I saw Richard again, I knew how much I'd romanticised the memories.'

'Only I'd no idea of that. From everything you said, I thought you felt just the same about him. It was as much as I could do to be civil to the man. But apart from that I didn't like him. There was something about him I didn't trust, though it never occurred to me that he was capable of something as appalling as rape. Even when I saw the way he was acting towards you at the party, I thought it was jealousy that was making me paranoid. I should have backed my instincts, not let you leave with him and then immediately afterwards decide that I was uneasy about you being alone with him.'

Though it was a warm evening, Elise suddenly shivered. Luc drew her tightly against him, bringing her body into an intimate fit with his, his arms telling her that nothing and no one would ever hurt her again.

'It was a terrible evening all round,' she murmured, raising her head, her lips curving with a smile as she confessed, 'I'd spent the whole time on tenterhooks waiting for your engagement to be announced. I knew I was hopelessly in love with you. When Monsieur Charron proposed the second toast, I honestly thought my heart was going to break.'

Luc's eyes, a blaze in their depths, held hers as he answered, 'While all I wanted to do was to take you in my arms and kiss you till you couldn't remember your own name, let alone your ex-fiancé's!'

A glass-walled river-boat chugged past in mid-stream, and for a moment music drifted towards them on the breeze. But the magic was so strong between them that neither of them noticed. Elise linked her hands behind Luc's neck, the solitaire diamond engagement ring he had put on her finger a few hours before catching the lamplight. It flashed with sudden brilliance as Luc bent his head.

He kissed her long and ardently, moulding her to him, making an aching sweet longing course through her. Her pulses throbbed with excitement, need for him making her shiver. When finally he lifted his lips from hers, she knew from the flash of knowledge that swept between their eyes that they were both thinking the same thing.

Colour invaded her face, making her even prettier as she remembered his lovemaking that afternoon. He had alternated tenderness with hungry demand, till the ecstasy had built up to a fierce, mindless pleasure, and there was a sudden almost explosive release that had overwhelmed them both.

Huskily she said, 'Let's go back to our hotel room.'

'You mean you're tired?' he teased with a trace of devilment, before adding softly, 'I hope not, because I'm not going to let you sleep for a long time yet.'

Elise felt her pulse quicken. Her mind whirled for an instant as she thought of the future that lay ahead, of everything they would share in their intense, tempestuous relationship, and then it came back to tonight, a whole long glorious night of love and passion, the forerunner of countless such nights.

H A R L E Q U I N
Romance

Coming Next Month

#3061 ONE MORE SECRET Katherine Arthur
Writing detective stories as Joe Rocco was Kelsey's secret life, but could she keep it secret when Bart Malone appealed for Joe's help in a real mystery? Bart seemed hard to resist—but was there more than one mystery?

#3062 DANCING SKY Bethany Campbell
When Adam MacLaren, with his chain of modern discount stores, invades Dancing Sky, no one is safe. Not Mitzi's fiancé or the rest of the retailers. And least of all Mitzi. She finds herself singled out for the greatest upheaval of all.

#3063 PASSION'S FAR SHORE Madeleine Ker
Dorothy had accepted the job as governess to Pearl, not because she wanted to go to Japan, but because the little girl really needed her. But it seemed that Pearl's father, Calum Hescott, thought differently....

#3064 NO ACCOUNTING FOR LOVE Eva Rutland
Clay Kencade is a risk-taker. He's got a knack for business and a way with women. So why has he fallen for serious, reserved Cindy Rogers, who's as cautious in her personal life as she is in business?

#3065 FROZEN ENCHANTMENT Jessica Steele
Jolene was delighted at the unexpected offer of traveling to Russia with the boss of Templeton's as his temporary secretary. But she soon discovered it was not going to be such fun, for Cheyne Templeton had already made up his mind what kind of girl Jolene was....

#3066 MASTER OF CASHEL Sara Wood
Caitlin resented Jake Ferriter for taking her beloved home, Cashelkerry, and blamed him for causing her father's death. But she could not deny the attraction she felt for this enigmatic, ruthless man. The feeling was mutual— but could she cope with his offer of an affair without commitment....

Available in June wherever paperback books are sold, or through Harlequin Reader Service:

In the U.S.
901 Fuhrmann Blvd.
P.O. Box 1397
Buffalo, N.Y. 14240-1397

In Canada
P.O. Box 603
Fort Erie, Ontario
L2A 5X3

Harlequin Regency Romance™

Romance the way it was *always* meant to be!

The time is 1811, when a Regent Prince rules the empire. The place is London, the glittering capital where rakish dukes and dazzling debutantes scheme and flirt in a dangerously exciting game. Where marriage is the passport to wealth and power, yet every girl hopes secretly for love....

Welcome to Harlequin Regency Romance where reading is an adventure and romance is *not* just a thing of the past! Two delightful books a month.

Available wherever Harlequin Books are sold.

Coming in July
From America's favorite author

JANET DAILEY

Fiesta San Antonio

Out of print since 1978!

The heavy gold band on her finger proved it was actually true. Natalie was now Mrs. Colter Langton! She had married him because her finances and physical resources for looking after her six-year-old nephew, Ricky, were rapidly running out, and she was on the point of exhaustion. He had married her because he needed a housekeeper and somebody to look after his young daughter, Missy. In return for the solution to her problems, she had a bargain to keep.

It wouldn't be easy. Colter could be so hard and unfeeling. "I don't particularly like myself," he warned her. "It's just as well you know now the kind of man I am. That way you won't expect much from our marriage."

If Natalie had secretly hoped that something would grow between them— the dream faded with his words. Was he capable of love?

Don't miss any of Harlequin's three-book collection of Janet Dailey's novels each with a Texan flavor. Look for *BETTER OR WORSE* coming in September, and if you missed *NO QUARTER ASKED*...

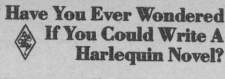

Have You Ever Wondered If You Could Write A Harlequin Novel?

Here's great news—Harlequin is offering a series of cassette tapes to help you do just that. Written by Harlequin editors, these tapes give practical advice on how to make your characters—and your story—come alive. There's a tape for each contemporary romance series Harlequin publishes.

Mail order only

All sales final

TO: *Harlequin Reader Service*
Audiocassette Tape Offer
P.O. Box 1396
Buffalo, NY   14269-1396

I enclose a check/money order payable to HARLEQUIN READER SERVICE® for $9.70 ($8.95 plus 75¢ postage and handling) for EACH tape ordered for the total sum of $_____*
Please send:

☐ Romance and Presents   ☐ Intrigue
☐ American Romance   ☐ Temptation
☐ Superromance   ☐ All five tapes ($38.80 total)

Signature_____

Name:_____ (please print clearly)

Address:_____

State:_____ Zip:_____

*Iowa and New York residents add appropriate sales tax.

AUDIO-H

HARLEQUIN
American Romance

THE LOVES OF A CENTURY...

Join American Romance in a nostalgic look back at the Twentieth Century—at the lives and loves of American men and women from the turn-of-the-century to the dawn of the year 2000.

Journey through the decades from the dance halls of the 1900s to the discos of the seventies ... from Glenn Miller to the Beatles ... from Valentino to Newman ... from corset to miniskirt ... from beau to Significant Other.

Relive the moments ... recapture the memories.

Look now for the CENTURY OF AMERICAN ROMANCE series in Harlequin American Romance. In one of the four American Romance titles appearing each month, for the next twelve months, we'll take you back to a decade of the Twentieth Century, where you'll relive the years and rekindle the romance of days gone by.

Don't miss a day of the CENTURY OF AMERICAN ROMANCE.

A CENTURY OF
AMERICAN ROMANCE
1900's

The women...the men...the passions...
the memories....

CAR-1